Fantasy Annual 3

New stories of science fiction and fantasy

edited by

Philip Harbottle and Sean Wallace

Cosmos Books

A COSMOS BOOK
First edition: December 1999

ISBN: 0-9668968-2-3
Library of Congress Catalog Card Number: 99-067451

Cosmos Books are published by Philip Harbottle / Cosmos Literary Agency, 32 Tynedale Avenue, Wallsend, Tyne and Wear, NE28 9LS, England and Sean Wallace, 589 Park Hill Avenue, Fairlawn, OH 44333, USA, and printed and distributed by Lightning Print, a subdivision of Ingrams Book Group, USA. All purchase orders should be sent to Philip Harbottle (UK) and Sean Wallace (US).

CONTENTS

FALLEN ANGEL

by E. C. Tubb

A flash of rose, a scent, a voice which echoed in the hollows of his mind and, suddenly, he was alive again. Fully alive, really alive, not lying on a slab while instruments probed and delved, measured and indexed, twisted and tested. Not writhing in torment as muscle and nerve and sinew were strained to the limits of endurance and then pushed further beyond. Alive and well and soon to be free. Free!

The concept was intoxicating as the drink and drugs he had once known which had rotted his brain and body in return for a brief euphoria. He sat and thought about it in the place where he was kept. A mist swirled about the area moulding itself into the illusion that he sat on a bench of stone, in a chamber of stone scented with the perfume of hidden blooms. Soon now, he would see real flowers, walk again in sunlight, feel the wind, the rain, the touch of snow. To eat genuine food, talk to real people, forget what had happened if forgetting was possible.

"It is," said the alien. "Most things are." He had appeared as he always did, abruptly, seated, a tall, lean, white-haired man looking, in his simple robe, like an ancient Greek philosopher. It was a facade. An illusion to mask the true shape of the creature. "But no interference on our part will be necessary," he continued. "Your race has a peculiar ability to ignore the unpleasant. The defensive application of a highly selective memory."

"Yes," said Frank. He could believe it. Once he had seen the creature as it really was. Now it was almost impossible to accept that such a thing could actually exist. "I was told that I was to be released. Am I?"

"Of course, Mr. Engel. We do not lie." The classical features creased into a smile. "You probably feared that we would eliminate you but we have no reason for that. You may not realise it but we have much to thank you for. You have been most co-operative. With your assistance we have gained much knowledge of your world and we shall learn more. We are grateful."

Grateful! Would a fisherman talk that way to a creature he had hauled from the water, cut open, looked at, sewn up and was ready to throw back into the sea? Maybe if the fish could talk but would he give it a reward?

"It is our custom," said the alien. The words echoed without vibration, a soft tingling impinging directly on the cortex. "Our ethics forbid us to take without giving something in return. The device is one much used among us for social convenience. It is an eraser. With it you can undo a mistake. Gain the advantage of a second chance. Avoid unpleasant situations. You should find it most useful."

"Sure," said Frank. "But—" He broke off for the alien had gone, the room, the swirling mist and walls of apparent stone. He still sat but the bench was of wood. The air carried the scent of visible flowers. There was sound; the sigh of wind, the rustle of leaves, the shouts of children at play. And, all around, the bright warmth of a summer sun.

Summer? It had been winter when he'd been taken, cold, hungry, dying, without a job, a home, a friend, a shred of hope. The way a man gets when the money runs out and the drink and the drugs and nothing is left but hunger, the pain of diseased lungs and the ravages of dissipation. He'd been a good specimen for the aliens. Who would miss him? Who would believe him? Who would he want to convince?

No one. He was cured and he knew it. No more addiction. No more disease. A good chance to make a fresh start. He knew what needed to be done and he had the alien's gift to help him do it.

He sat and looked at it, eyes narrowed against reflected sunshine. Beside him a man stirred in his sleep smelling of staleness but human because of it. Just one of the drifters who thronged the park. Across the gravelled path another bench held three others, two old, one a kid with a waxen face and twitching hands. One of the men rose, stretched, headed down the path. Frank ignored him, concentrating on the gift.

It was a ring, the band thick, wide, raised in one part, a prominence that could be pressured by the impact of the adjoining finger. The jewel was a large, domed, ruby-like stone striated with what could have been a diffraction grating. Frank was a social failure but not an idiot and some things were obvious. The ring was more than an ornament but just what he didn't know. The alien hadn't explained. He examined it again, studying the protuberance. He pressed it.

Nothing happened.

Nothing, that is, aside from the fact that the man who had risen from the facing bench and who had walked down the path was abruptly sitting on the bench again. As Frank watched he rose, stretched and walked away. The stud on the ring sank beneath the squeeze of his finger. Nothing happened. He waited, tried again—and the man was back on the bench. He rose, stretched, walked down the path exactly as he had done twice before. This time Frank let him go.

He knew now what the alien had given him.

He leaned back filled with the wonder of it. An eraser, the alien had said. A device for social convenience. A thing with which to undo a mistake and to gain another chance. It was something you could need to use quickly, easily, have close all the time. What could be more convenient than a ring? A very special kind of ring. A neat device, he thought, looking at it. Compact, ornamental, unobtrusive, probably everlasting.

A one-way time machine.

* * * * * * * *

The main-line station housed a throng of travellers. Frank ignored them all as he concentrated on the large digital clock. The figures read 18.02. He activated the ring. The figures changed to 17.05. Fifty-seven seconds, the same as twice before. He made more experiments. Activated the ring threw you back in time, but you had to wait fifty-seven seconds before it could be activated again. No accumulation. The stud could be kept depressed and there would be an automatic activation. Nothing you carried less than fifty-seven seconds in the past went back with you. It was all he needed to know.

The crossing lights were at red. Frank, distracted, stepped from the kerb directly into the path of a heavy truck. Brakes screamed, a woman, a man. A moment of panic then his fingers closed and he was instantly back on the sidewalk heading towards the crossing. He checked with his watch. Fifty-seven seconds. Call it a minute. He paused, waited for the truck to pass, the lights to change to green.

A minute.

Not long? Try holding your breath that long. Try resting your rear on a hot stove for half that time. In a minute you can walk a hundred yards, run almost a quarter of a mile, fall three. You can conceive, die, get married. A minute is time enough for a lot of things.

Frank closed his hand and looked at the ring. Thinking. Take the classical situation. A couple, the man old, the woman young. You greet them, assume the woman is the old man's daughter, discover she is his wife. Loss of equanimity, and the generation of embarrassment. So activate and go back in time. Meet the couple again but now armed with knowledge. Politeness reigns. In any society such a device would be in demand.

But not for soothing an old man's ego. Not just for that.

Not when he had no job, nowhere to live, an ache for luxury in his belly and a yen for the good life in his soul. He had drawn on the experience of three decades of tough living to get a wristwatch and decent shoes and clothing. But he still needed money.

A liquor store shone down the street, a bright cavern filled with bottled dreams. Frank leaned close to the window, squinting against the lights, staring inside and checking what he saw. The place seemed deserted, the owner probably busy out back. A cash register stood on the counter flanked by stacked cans. He waited, counting seconds. A minute and a half and no sign of life. He activated, walked into the store, operated the cash register and took out a thin sheaf of bills. He was almost at the door when the owner appeared. A big, beefy man with a balding head and savage eyes. He came charging from a room at the rear shouting and waving a baseball bat.

"Hold it you! Move and I'll smash your head in!"

He meant it. Frank squeezed the ring—nothing happened.

Nothing would happen until the time was up. He had to stall.

"Now listen," he said. "It's not like it seems. It's a publicity stunt, see? Just for advertising. You'll—"

"By God, the nerve of it!" The owner came closer, lifting the club, snarling his hate. "A stinking thief walks in and robs the till, then gives you a load of mouth. I'll give you mouth! I'll give you a damned sight more than that!"

Frank squeezed his fingers keeping the stud depressed as he dived to one side. The owner was fast. The club slammed against the edge of the door then followed him down. He felt and heard the crack of bone as it slammed against his knee. He rolled as it lifted for another blow—and he was leaning against the window the glass cool against his brow. He fought to control his breath. He was safe, his knee uninjured, the store seemingly deserted.

Mopping sweat he felt the bloom of anger. The bastard had tried to kill him. To smash in his skull for the sake of a little cash. He would be lounging in his room, watching television, enjoying something to eat. He'd have a gimmick rigged to the door to signal when anyone came in. That, and maybe a mirror to watch the till. Nursing his club and aching to use it. The blood-crazed slob! He had it coming!

Again he entered the empty store and operated the register but this time, instead of heading for the door, snatched up a bottle and moved to the rear. As the owner appeared he swung at the balding skull. The bottle shattered into a mass of sparkling fragments mixed with a flood of wine, blood and spattered brain. He dropped the neck and scooped up the club. The shape of a wallet bulged the rear pocket of the dead man's jeans. He bent, dragged it free, flipped it open and saw a wad of bills. Straightening he thrust it into a pocket and strode towards the door. A looming shadow blocked the opening.

Quickly he rammed his foot against the panel.

"Sorry. We're closed."

"I want a drink. I gotta have a drink." The voice was a begging whine. "I got money, see?" A hand lifted, waving a crumpled note. "Just a bottle of something cheap."

A lush and close to desperation. Frank recognised the danger. To lock him out was to invite curses, broken windows, unwanted attention. To let him in was to give him a view of murder.

He activated the ring and was standing by the till cash in his hand. Quickly he reached for a bottle and moved to the rear. This time he didn't smash in the owner's skull but swung hard and low at the belly and groin. He took the wallet from where he knew it would be. The club remained where it had fallen. He thrust the bottle into the hands of the lush at the door. Outside a cab halted at his signal.

"Where to?"

"A casino. A good one." Frank relaxed against the cushions as the driver glided from the kerb. "Waste no time, friend. I feel lucky."

* * * * * * * *

Luck, the fortuitous combination of favourable circumstances, but who needs luck when they know what will happen fifty-seven seconds in advance? Long enough for the dice to settle, the card to turn, the ball to drop. The winner to win. The ability to make quick, impulsive, apparently stupid last-second wagers against a seemingly sure thing. Frank rode high, a sure-fire winner.

In more ways than one.

He stretched, enjoying the shower, the impact of water driven at high pressure against hair and skin massaging and stimulating as it tightened tissue and stung flesh into an exhilarating awareness. He turned a control and gasped as the water turned into a frigid goose-pimpling medium. A titillation as many things were now thanks to the alien gift and his own aptitude. He jerked the control back to hot, waited, then cut the spray and stepped from the shower drying himself on a fluffy towel.

"Frank, darling. Are you going to be much longer?"

A female voice with the peculiar intonation of the inbred upper classes; a member of the aristocracy by birth and a failed marriage. The Lady Jane Smyth-Connors was rich, decadent, bored and a problem.

"A moment, honey," he called and dropped the towel. A mirror reflected a pleasing image. Money had improved on what the aliens had accomplished; cosmetic magic smoothing away accumulated blemishes, the scars of his early days. He'd worked hard to gain the physique of an athlete. He had been born with a pleasing face. Money had taken care of other things, his clothes, his accent, the education of his tastes. He had become a fringe-member of the jet-set. Rich. Handsome. Riding high. Saddled now with a crippled bird.

"Frank? Come to me!"

"Give me a moment." He resisted the instinctive rush of anger at the tone, the command. She was arrogant and domineering but that had been obvious from the start. He had met her in a casino, recognising the desperation of a woman who wanted to win but could only lose. Recognising, too, an echo of what he had once been. The opportunity she presented. He had made a point of meeting her and she'd been attracted by his looks, figure and calculated attention. Now, invited to her home, perfectly obvious of what was expected, he stood on the edge of respectable security.

The bathroom had a window. He parted the curtains and looked into the night. Way down low a scatter of lights carpeted the misty ground. London was a nice city. England a nice place. Very nice, especially to gamblers—no tax was levied on winnings. Here, more than anywhere else, high prizes were to be won. Not just money, that was for the plebeians, but make the right connections and every day would be Christmas.

"Frank!"

Fretful impatience and the imperious tone of one accustomed to instant obedience. The woman waited to be served. Sighing he entered the bedroom.

She was a little older than himself, tall with a peculiar angularity, giving the impression of an overgrown schoolgirl, who should be wearing tweeds and wielding a hockey stick. The appearance was deceptive. Generations of inbreeding had done more than fashion the distribution of flesh and bone. It had developed a festering degeneracy. She was, he knew, almost clinically insane but, in her class, people were never insane only 'eccentric', never stupid only 'amusing', never spiteful, savage, vicious or cruel only 'thoughtless'.

He reached out and took her into his arms and kissed her with educated skill. He ran his hands over her body, silk rustling as it fell from her naked flesh. Gently he bit the base of her throat, harder, felt her tense, her negative reaction.

"No," she snapped. "I hate anyone doing that!"

One bad mark. He counted seconds as he reached for the light switch. With darkness she squirmed, pushed herself free of his embrace.

"I hate the dark! Must you be like all the others?"

Two bad marks. Twenty seconds to go. Time for one more exploration. His hands reached out, made contact, moved with studied determination. She sighed with mounting pleasure.

"Frank—my angel!"

He activated the ring.

Reaching out he took her in his arms this time making no attempt to nibble or bite. Her clothing rustled to the floor and her skin gleamed with a nacreous sheen. He looked at her with bold admiration and his hands moved in the way he had learned gave her pleasure.

She closed her eyes, fingernails digging into his back. "Talk to me," she demanded. "Talk to me!"

He began counting seconds.

Later, as she lay in satiated slumber, he rested, thinking, planning, oddly amused. He had been the perfect lover. He had said and done all the things she had wanted in the exact order she had wanted them and, most important, without her having to instruct him at any time. He had been a reflection, an echo of her complex needs, and why not? He had worked hard to map the blueprint of her desire. Exploring, investigating, erasing all false starts and mistakes. Doing and saying nothing which had been unwelcome.

What else could he be for her but perfect?

He turned, looking down at the woman, seeing her not just as flesh and blood but as a soul in desperate need. A mass of conflicting emotions and frustrated needs, one not to be used but to be helped.

She sighed, opened her eyes, looked up at the face of her lover. "My angel! My darling!"

He said what she wanted him to say.

She sighed again, same sound, different meaning. "I've never been so happy. I can't believe this is happening." Her fingers trailed over his arm, his hand, halted at the ring. "Why do you wear this? It's so big. So heavy. It looks like a knuckle-duster. Is it for protection?"

"In a way."

"I'll protect you," she said, then added, musingly: "Your name suits you. Engel, that's German for angel. Frank means honest. You are a frank angel. Are you an honest one?"

"I try to be."

"Then I'll give you a treat. Tonight I'll take you to a party. You'll love it. There will be people it will help you to meet and all sorts of things to amuse you."

Drugs and drink and he could guess the rest. "No."

"Why not? Don't be so staid, darling. Everyone needs to relax at times. We'll take a trip into paradise."

"No," he said again and added, "I can't stop you doing what you want but I've been where you're heading for and I don't recommend it. Anyway, I can't see you tonight."

"Why not?" Jealousy reared her upright. "I need you. You know that. Why can't I see you? You said—"

"I know what I said and I meant every word of it. I love you to distraction, darling, but I have to fly to New York. Business," he added. "After all I do have to make a living."

She said, quickly, "You don't have to worry about that, darling. I'll speak to Daddy and—"

He closed her lips with his own. "I still have to go to New York," he insisted. Against her naked body his hands did what she wanted them to do. "And later, after I return—"

"We'll get married," she said. "I never want to lose you."

Christmas, he thought, as dawn paled the sky.

* * * * * * * *

The plane was big, sleek, beautiful with matching flight attendants all breasts and legs and eyes and silken hair with a 'you may look at me because I'm beautiful but you must never, ever touch' attitude. A machine offering the ultimate in comfort for those willing to pay for it. Frank was willing and able and travelled luxury class. Room for everyone with plenty to spare and he was glad of it.

He felt tired. The night had been hectic and the morning little better. It was good to sit and relax neatly strapped in a form-fitting chair as the jets gulped air and spewed it behind in a man-made hurricane which sent the plane down the runway and up into the air. London fell away, a misty blur, the clouds dropped like tufts of dirty cotton and then there was only the sun, a watchful eye in an immense iris of blue.

He liked to travel and a little absence could make a heart grow fonder and, for him, there was a kick in flying. He liked to look down and think of all the emptiness between him and the ground. Feel his stomach tighten with acrophobia, the delicious sensation of fear experienced in perfect safety. Height had no meaning on a plane. All you had to do was to look straight ahead and you could be in a train. A Pullman, naturally, nothing but the best was good enough for the winners in this world.

And he was one of them. Wealthy and soon to be married to a rich and doting woman who had all the right connections. One for whom he felt an unexpected fondness. He would be fair taking nothing she wasn't willing to give. He didn't have to. Not if what he planned worked out.

He unstrapped, stretched his legs, glanced through a window as the captain's voice came over the speakers telling anyone interested of their height and velocity. Through the pane he could see very little. The sky, the clouds below, the tip of a wing. Old stuff. The blonde attendant was far from that. She swayed among the seats, caught his eye, responded with instant attention. Was he quite comfortable? Would he like a pillow? A newspaper? A magazine? Something to drink?

"Brandy," he said. "With ice and soda."

He sat on an inner seat close to the wall of the cabin so that she had to step from the aisle in order to lower the flap and set down his drink. He lifted his left hand and touching her knee, slid his palm slowly up the inside of her thigh. He felt her stiffen and saw the expression on her face, a compound of incredulity, outrage, interest and speculation. Automatically he counted the seconds. Fifty-four...five...six...

He pressed the stud on his ring.

The tray made a little thudding sound as it came to rest, the brandy a liquid gurgling as it gushed from the miniature bottle over the ice. She smiled, gesturing with the punctured can of soda. "All of it, sir?"

He nodded, watching as she poured, remembering the soft warmth of her thigh, the yielding temptation of her flesh. Knowing he had touched her only because it was forbidden. A stupid, childish thing to have done and totally unnecessary. If he wanted her she was available, her body language had made that clear. Did she know what he had done? No, he decided as she moved away. To her nothing had happened. She had served him a drink and that was all. But—?

Brooding he stared at the ring. You activated it and went back fifty-seven seconds in time. All you had done during that period was erased. You could do anything you liked and none of it mattered because it had all been cancelled. But it had been real. He remembered the pulped skull of the liquor store owner. A murder cancelled but it had happened. He could remember it. Could you remember what had never taken place?

"Sir?" The stewardess was back, smiling, some magazines in her hand. "I thought these might interest you," she said. "I picked a range. Would you care for another drink? The same as before? Right away, sir."

She gave it to him and swayed across the cabin as he reached for the magazines. Naked women ogled at him from the pages of a soft-porn publication and he wondered why she had chosen it. To hint that she was far from being a prude? To arouse his interest? To test his sexuality? His interest? Checking him out in her own way as he had done Jane the previous night. But he had no interest in pictured nudity.

The magazine fell to one side as he reached for a different publication. One dealing with oddities of nature and science and strong on the occult. He flipped pages, pausing to read, interested despite his cynicism. One article in particular held his attention.

According to the author some fifteen million Americans claimed to have been abducted by aliens, tested, interfered with, examined and then released with only the vaguest of memories of what they claimed had happened.

So he was not alone.

Yet if he could remember why couldn't they? Had their

experience been based on nothing but mass hysteria? Wishful thinking? A simple desire to break out of faceless conformity. Had each received a gift? Could they be recognised by the rings they could be wearing?

He looked at his own knowing it was not what it seemed. But was it more? He leaned back, thinking, remembering the calm figure in the simple robe. The explanation he had been given. Closing his eyes he made a mental journey back in time, feeling the stone of the bench, the flower-scented mist. Seeing the figure dressed in a simple robe the alien resembling an ancient Greek philosopher. What had he said?

"You may not realise it, Mr. Engel, but we have much to thank you for. You have been most co-operative. With your assistance we have gained much knowledge of your world and we shall learn more."

Learn more? How?

The ring—it had to be the ring. It swelled in his vision the stone a baleful eye. A time machine—but what else? A recorder? A transmitter? A tracking device? Had it monitored each activation? Was it a continuation of his physical examination? A means to test his moral fibre? Turning him into a representative sample of what could be expected from any of his species?

If so they would learn how strong curiosity was to the human race. How tempting wealth and power. His business in New York was to meet experts in computer technology and other fields. Those who could scan the ring with specialised techniques, testing, prying, monitoring in order to determine the composition of the metal, the stone, its design and molecular structure. If it could be copied he would gain wealth beyond the dreams of avarice.

And he would have given freedom to the teeming inhabitants of an increasingly violent world. A defence against attack and injury. A means of escape from disasters and unthinking acts of violence. Had the aliens guessed what he intended?

He lifted his hand and stared into the stone. The ring was his to do with as he pleased. A gift. A thing given him by something resembling an ancient Greek and he remembered a cogent statement learned when young. "Beware the Greeks when they come bearing gifts."

But not this one. It had given him stature. The chance of social enhancement. Of confirmed social security but it could give him what he still lacked, the unquestioning power of incredible wealth.

The plane rocked a little. The voice from the speaker was calm, unhurried. "Will all passengers please fasten their safety belts. We are heading into an area of minor turbulence. You may see a little lightning but there is absolutely nothing to worry about. We are, of course, flying well above the area of storm."

The blonde came through the cabin, tutted when she saw his unfastened belt and made it fast. As she walked away he reached for the magazine, wondering if, in the letter column, there could be a claim from someone who had something concrete to show for their claimed meeting with aliens. The magazine fell from his lap to one side beyond his reach. Impatiently he released the safety belt and picked up the publication.

It held nothing of interest. Smiling at the stewardess he gestured for her to fetch him another drink.

Something hit the roof of the cabin. There was a ripping sound, a blast of air, an irresistible force which tore him from his seat and flung him into space. Air gushed from his lungs as he began to fall. He gulped, trying to breathe, to understand. Arctic chill numbed his flesh. He twisted, saw through streaming eyes the jagged gash in the fuselage, the shattered wreckage of the tail.

An accident, he thought wildly. A fireball, a meteor, metal fatigue even. A crack in the cabin wall and internal pressure would do the rest. And now he was falling. Falling!

His fingers squeezed in frenzied reaction.

"Please, sir." The blonde came towards him as he reared to his feet. "You must remain seated with your safety belt fastened unless—"

"Listen!" He grabbed her by both arms. "Tell the pilot to change course. Tell him now. Hurry!"

A fireball or meteor could be avoided. They would be safe if the course was changed fast enough. But it had to be done now. Now!

"Quick!" He ran towards the flight deck the girl at his heels. Damn the stupid bitch! Couldn't she understand? "This is an emergency!" he shouted. "Change course immediately!"

Something hit the roof of the cabin. The compartment ripped

open, metal coiling like the peeled skin of a banana. The blonde vanished. The shriek of tearing metal was lost in the explosive gusting of escaping air. Desperately Frank clung to a seat. He felt his hands torn from the fabric, his body sucked towards the opening. Once again he was ejected into space to begin the long, stomach-wrenching five-mile fall.

"No!" he screamed his terror. "Dear God, no!"

He activated.

"Please, sir, I really must insist! You must allow me to fasten your safety belt."

He was standing by his seat and the blonde was showing signs of getting annoyed. Annoyed!

"This is important," he said, fighting to remain calm. Ignoring the stares of the other passengers all neatly belted in their seats. "In less than a minute this plane is going to fall apart. Do something about it!"

Why did she stand there looking so dumb?

"You stupid cow, get out of my way!" He pushed her to one side and lunged towards the flight deck. "Change course!" he yelled. "For God's sake—"

Something hit the roof of the cabin. Again the roar, the blast, the irresistible force. Something struck his head and blurred his senses. He activated and found himself still in the open gulping at rarefied air and shivering in the savage cold. To one side, far lower, the shattered plane hung in a cloud of dissipating wreckage. Tiny fragments hung around it one of them, perhaps, the blonde.

Below the sea spread in a shimmer of light and water. His stomach constricted with the overwhelming terror of acrophobia as he stared at the waves. Imagining the moment of inevitable impact. Falling he would die ten thousand deaths in cringing anticipation.

Spasmodically he clamped his fingers tightly together against the ring. Immediately he was high in the air again with almost a minute of grace in which to fall.

Fifty-seven seconds...repeated...repeated...repeated...repeated... repeated...

Falling, endlessly falling.

An angel suspended between Heaven and Earth.

THE BURROWERS

by David Somers

Fletcher identified with the mole as it bored through rock and ice. The cabin was cramped, filled with dials and gauges, pipes and cables and levers. It smelt of hot oil. He watched the scanner as the slowly rotating blades of the screw churned into rock, engine whining in protest, seat vibrating. Sonar reflected only rock ahead.

He compared his actual route with the plan; this shift was going well. He felt snug in his cabin, like an animal in its nest. Unlike some of the younger drivers, he took an interest in the job; it wasn't just routine drilling for pay. He frowned; why, if the youngsters weren't concentrating on the job, was it older men who had the accidents? It didn't seem fair.

He studied the bubble gauge to check his level; dead straight and horizontal; no problem, bang on specification. He looked at the clock; on schedule too. Behind him, a lining machine crawled, securing roof and walls.

There came a grating noise and, without warning, the mole lurched forward, the screw's cutting edge biting vacuum. Cursing, he grabbed the emergency brake. Too late. He tried to reverse. No go. Traction lost, the tracks spun idly. The screen showed a gap where the rock face had been. Breakthrough!

Rock had changed to ice, shattered and collapsed above a void. The mole tilted, balanced on the brink of the drop. It seesawed, sliding forward. Fletcher had never felt so helpless. Darkness swallowed him and he screamed as he fell...

* * * * * * * *

"There's Ariel now," Dr. Nile said.

Uranus hung large through a porthole of the supply ship, a greenish-blue sphere partly obscured by cloud. At this distance, the rings were visible. The satellite looked lumpy, cratered and criss-crossed with faults and fractures. It didn't look a friendly sort of place to make a home. Well, with luck, he wouldn't be staying long.

Dr. Barony said, irritation in her voice, "I have twenty-twenty vision, thank you."

"Just making conversation."

"Don't," she said. "I'm not interested. I'm here to do a job, that's all."

Nile forced a smile. "But we're here on the same job. Surely we can co-operate?"

She looked up at him, and away. He felt ridiculously tall beside her; intellectually inclined, he had no small talk for social moments, and Barony fascinated him. He was aware of her perfume, the dazzle of teeth against dark and shiny skin, her massive chest. He thought she must have the lungs of an opera singer. He was also aware of her prickly character.

"We're both here to help accident victims."

"Do you think so?" Her speech held a sing-song rhythm. "I thought we were drafted here to save expensive machinery and get the project back on schedule."

"I think you're being too hard on the Authority," Nile said, remembering she was a prominent Pro-Lifer.

The ship descended, touched the moon's surface with a bump and matched airlocks. Nile and Barony descended ladders to the hold. A cold chill seeped through and he realised just how inhospitable this moon was. He moved warily in a weak gravity. Beyond the second lock, a blast of heated air struck him. A tunnel, brilliantly lit, stretched away downwards.

A man, wearing a white one-piece coverall, waited to greet them. His face was craggy as granite, his expression calm.

"Welcome to Ariel, Dr. Barony. Welcome, Dr. Nile. My name is Ramsay and I'm the Expeditor. This way, please. Our unloaders need every bit of room for moving supplies—your luggage will be delivered to your quarters."

Footsteps and voices echoed along the tunnel. Nile blinked; lighting was too harsh for comfort, the air hot and stuffy. They passed chambers without doors but, every few hundred metres, was an airlock.

They turned into a side tunnel that led to a large chamber. Helmeted operators sat before screens, gripping control levers.

"Our Operations Centre," Ramsay said, gesturing at a three-D map against one curving wall. "I brought you here first because I want you to see what you're up against. Each operator controls a mole by telemetry, and the whole operation is devoted to cutting tunnels and chambers into this moon.

"Building living and working space aboard the first generation ship to travel to the stars is what Ariel is all about. This is a long-term project aimed at finding alien life. We believe there is intelligence out there and that we can learn from it."

He paused. "Now we're falling behind schedule, and some operators suffer trauma. Expensive machines are lost—"

"How are they lost?" Nile asked.

"Ariel is close to twelve hundred kilometres in diameter—you can work out the volume yourself. Remember we are surface creatures and never really appreciate the sheer internal size of a sphere.

"Ariel is already honeycombed with natural caverns and tunnels and shafts; that's why it was chosen. Despite sonar, a breakthrough into a cavity can be unexpected. And if it happens to be a vertical shaft, the mole falls god knows how far into the interior. It's lost to us anyway—and if the operator is slow withdrawing, he falls with it and suffers trauma."

Barony said, "Are you sure it's because of an imaginary fall? The operator is safe in this room. Could it be due to a virus natural to this moon?"

"We're not sure of anything," Ramsay admitted. "That's why you've been invited to investigate. You, Dr. Barony, to test for micro-organisms, and Dr. Nile to check for brain lesions."

"And you, of course," said Barony, turning to look up at Nile, "are sure it'll be all in the mind."

"Brain," he corrected. "Forget about mind. First we need to collect what facts are available; theory can come later."

She turned away without replying. Nile stared around the chamber, at the helmeted operators, each intent on controlling his own mole. "Now I'd like to see the latest victim."

Ramsay nodded. "His name's Fletcher and he's in our sick bay. This way..."

They returned to the main corridor and entered another side tunnel. The sick bay was at the end and, like all hospital wards, smelt of antiseptic. The lighting was subdued and individual cubicles soundproofed.

Barony paused to question the duty nurse. Ramsay went directly to one man sitting alone; he held a mirror and stared at his reflection.

"Mr. Fletcher. This is Dr. Nile – he's come all the way from Earth to help you."

The patient continued to gaze into his mirror with wide hollowed eyes. "So?" His voice was so low that Nile had to bend close to understand him. "I keep telling you, I won't go back. I've finished with tunnelling."

"You don't have to," Ramsay said quietly. "You're officially retired. When your pension arrangements have been completed, you'll be returned home."

"White," Fletcher mumbled. He laid down his mirror and, for the first time, peered at Nile. "Hair's white. Last time I looked it was just starting to turn grey."

"Shock sometimes does that." Nile pulled up a chair and sat down. "But you didn't fall, Mr. Fletcher. You weren't even in the machine."

"Slaved to a machine. You don't know what it's like. Feels like you're there...can't face it. Nightmares. The breakthrough, the emptiness beyond...like nothing...swallowing you." He shivered. "You should try it."

"Perhaps I will," Nile said mildly. "Thank you for talking to me, Mr. Fletcher."

Barony joined them. "They still haven't found a biological cause, but I've brought some new drugs with me to try out." She glanced at Ramsay. "Is there anyone who fell but wasn't traumatised?"

"Yes. I'll introduce you when he comes off shift."

The Expeditor escorted them to their quarters and proposed meeting later for a meal. "It will be easier for Jennings if it doesn't seem a formal interview. Just follow the pale blue arrows to the dining room."

Nile sniffed. "There's a strong chemical smell."

"Organic chemicals," Barony corrected.

Nile's rooms were spacious with smooth pastel-coloured walls; furnishings were extruded plastic. The bed was low and wide enough for two and he imagined Barony stretched out on it. He washed, changed and followed the pale blue arrows.

The dining room was large and noisy and he saw Ramsay wave from a table tucked away in a corner. He collected a tray of hot food from a self-service counter.

Barony, wearing large gold earrings that swayed and glittered with every movement of her body was chatting with a young man. Ramsay introduced them.

"Mr. Jennings—Dr. Nile, a neuro-scientist from Earth."

Jennings nodded, not really interested; his admiring gaze left Barony only briefly.

She was speaking. "Mr. Ramsay confirms it is the older operators who get trapped in their helmets. Why is this, do you think? Slower reaction times? Did you feel all right immediately before your machine fell? You hadn't caught a bug, for instance?"

"I felt fine," Jennings said. "I reckon the older operators can't adapt quickly, the way we can. I'm okay so long as I remember I'm not really there. Older drivers still tend to cling to a belief in an individual mind."

"That's interesting," Nile said. "Fletcher suggested I should try driving a mole—to get the feeling of it."

"He's right there," Jennings said. "Unless you drive one, you can't appreciate how real it gets."

Nile nodded, convinced. "I'll do it," he said.

Barony laughed. "This I have to see!"

Next shift, Ramsay supervised his basic training. Nile sat in a control chair in the Ops Centre, hands gripping metal levers, watching a screen.

"We'll start you well back from the rock face," Ramsay said, "to give you time to get used to the mole. You'll find it easy enough to drive along a lined tunnel. When you reach the face, slow down till the cutting blade engages. Go slow. Give yourself time to get the feel of it. Ignore the noise; concentrate on your instruments."

Behind him, Nile heard Barony's earrings jangle as she tossed her head. "Waste of time and resources...like a small boy with a new toy. I'm away to see Mr. Fletcher."

"Are you sure you want to go through with this?" Ramsay asked.

"I'm sure."

"Okay. Watch your sonar. This is the brake; this gives you reverse. If you start a breakthrough, pull back quickly."

Ramsay lowered a helmet over his head and the last words he heard were "Connecting you *now*..."

Then he really was inside a mole. The levers felt smooth under his touch; he sensed vibration, smelt oil. Easing the machine forward, he gained confidence. When he reached the face his sonar registered solid rock. The cutting edge struck home with a shriek and a whine. He backed off and edged forward again.

It was too real. Now he could understand how drivers became trapped in their vehicles while burrowing deep underground.

He told himself, "I am not here, this is an illusion. Only the neurons firing in my brain back in the Operations Centre have any reality. Nothing else. I am not inside this machine."

He turned down the lighting and checked his instruments. Depth. Angle. He sensed himself relaxing, growing casual in his attitude, becoming over-confident and taking too much for granted. He repeated part of the neuroscientist's credo:

"I am the brain in the body.
This is my only reality..."

I'm not down here at all, he kept telling himself; this is illusion. But it still felt as if he was sitting in the driving seat of a mole, cutting rock, drilling a tunnel to help excavate this moon so that one day it would become the first starship. It was too convincing.

He dreamed a little. "What did you do aboard the Ariel, grandad?"

"I drove one of the moles."

Sudden cold enveloped him, bringing with it the icy chill of danger. A high-pitched shrilling indicated tortured machinery. The mole began rocking like a see-saw, wilder and wilder.

Christ, he had breakthrough! He was balanced on a knife-edge above a void, shivering with sweat running down his face. Brake didn't work; he tried to reverse and found he had no traction.

"Illusion!" he shouted. "This is an illusion." He tried desperately to believe his own words. "I am not here!"

A dark hole gaped like a mouth. He glimpsed stalactites, or were they teeth, descending? He was being swallowed along with his mole, disappearing into a vast mouth. He stabbed a finger at his searchlight control; the beam revealed the interior of a segmented body, a sea of churning acid.

He shuddered and screamed as he fell headlong into a stomach. "I do not believe this is happening! I believe..." He repeated aloud his credo:

"I will not fear: I am the brain in the body,
this is my only reality.
I am the gate that allows information to pass,
or denies it.
I am the parallel connections that provide
alternative pathways.
Mind is an illusion of the brain,
connecting neurons with the physical world beyond."

He felt calmer, in control. The helmet! He reached up to lift the helmet from his head and was immediately back in a chair in the Operations Centre.

Ramsay's voice sounded anxious: "Are you all right?"

Nile felt exhausted and short of breath. He sagged in the chair. "Quite an experience," he gasped. "Give me a moment and I'll explain."

He took large breaths, forced himself to relax taut muscles. He had never been in danger yet still his body denied this. He repeated the credo silently. Fletcher was right, he thought wryly; now I understand...

Barony handed him a glass of water and he gulped it down. It tasted fresh, not like the usual recycled stuff aboard ship. Well, there was plenty of ice out here.

He handed back the empty glass, smiling. "Thanks. The explanation is simple, if unexpected. We are not alone. Ariel has its own life and it's something like a giant worm. The tunnels honeycombing this satellite are wormholes. When a mole falls, it is into the mouth of a worm; small wonder that a driver slow to remove his helmet is traumatised."

"Worms!" Ramsay exclaimed. "We'll soon exterminate them."

"You won't!" Barony shouted. "I won't let you—all life is sacred, not just human."

Too late Ramsey remembered she was a Pro-Lifer. "Worms aren't intelligent—"

"So it's all right to destroy a simple life-form? We're going to the stars to find alien life, and here it is right under our noses. And all you can think of is kill it. Bloody arrogance!"

Ramsay eased his collar. "But the Authority is concerned with cost. We're losing machines, and work on Ariel is too far advanced to stop and start again on another moon."

"Really? We'll see about that when I've alerted the Pro-Lifers." Barony swung away, almost running to the communications centre.

Ramsay sighed. "As if I haven't enough problems."

"Perhaps not so many now," Nile said mildly. "I suggest using younger people as drivers—and extra time spent reinforcing the credo."

He paused. "And can we be sure Ariel's worms are not intelligent? If we could communicate with them, perhaps they will dig our tunnels for us! This ship could be on its way to the stars sooner than anyone imagined."

He nodded to Ramsay and followed after Barony. With one problem out of the way, perhaps he could concentrate on persuading her to see him in a more romantic light.

THE GULF

by Philip E. High

Sometimes they line the shore and stare out across the ocean. They are free to leave but none try. They know they can cross the water but, beyond, is a gulf which can never be bridged.

Behind the watchers lies the island, one hundred and eighty kilometres in length and approximately ninety wide. It is gentle, tropical, and, from its inception as a base, wholly self-supporting. Eight hundred and twenty one specialists and their families live here, funded by several highly technical nations.

It was known to be a base for intense research but the actual aim of the centre was never stated. It was only known that, one day, something went wrong with it. No one knew precisely what but the measures taken were warning enough. No one could enter and no one could leave. Constant naval patrols ensured that no one could approach it. Airspace above the island was a forbidden area with the threat of destruction to any craft defying the ban.

To all intents and purposes the island had become an infected area and members of the media seeking information were dealt with ruthlessly.

Relatives on the mainland were treated to a show by the involved nations. They 'deeply deplored the tragedy,' they arranged impressive church services and built memorials. Those bereaved were more than adequately compensated and all received free essential services and generous help for life.

No, sadly and with deep regret, it was not possible to collect the bodies for internment or cremation. It would be sometime before mankind could safely enter the area.

The media, needless to say, filled columns or programmes for weeks with speculation and alleged specialists who actually knew what had happened.

A special nuclear device had got out of hand and rendered the entire island radio-active.

A new nerve gas had—

A biological device had—

There can be no doubt that—

* * * * * * * * *

"You could be the first there, Peter my boy." Seager rolled the stub cigar from one side of his mouth to the other. "Look, you could be first in, get a scoop. Solve the mystery of the project that ended to tragically. I'll treble everything, salary, bonus, expenses, the lot. You're already a top reporter, this could make you forever. You could ask a thousand dollars a word anywhere and, as God's my judge, you'd get it without a quibble. We'll back you to the hilt, we can get a submarine in close, less than a nautical mile from the shore, below the radar sweep if there is one."

"Oh, very well, I'll go." What the hell, there was nobody who would grieve for him if anything happened. His mother had died five years ago, and he had never known his father. His mother had told him he'd been killed in an accident when he was only a few weeks old.

Peter felt his reporter's familiar sense of frustration. What project and what tragedy? Someone must know, some scientist or other must have gone in to see, to find out and finally report. Why the secrecy, what dreadful event needed such an unyielding wall of secrecy?

* * * * * * * * *

Seager had been as good as his word. God knew how but a submarine had, somehow, been pulled out the hat. Perhaps Seager's brother was an Admiral or something; anyway the submarine had been there. A too-genial bearded captain had shaken his hand vigorously and wished him luck.

"If they have radar over there, we're well below it. The sea is warm and the currents are in your favour. It will be a piece of cake, man, take my word for it."

Peter in his wet suit was prepared to vouch for some of it. The sea was warm, he could feel the current and, to help, he had one of the new mini-propulsion units attached to his suit. It was essential, he was also towing a pod of supplies, rations, recorders, change of clothing and, for reasons he didn't care to think about, a hand gun.

He thought, a nautical mile looks the hell of a distance, especially when one's chin is level with the ocean.

At long last the beach was drawing closer, golden in the sun, right for a tropical holiday, but to him—

Men must have felt like this storming the beaches in World War 2. The lovely sunlit beach held nothing but menace and if anything was lurking there, he was going to face it alone.

Sooner than he expected his feet were touching bottom and there was nowhere to go but forward. He walked up the warm sand, dragging the pod clear of the water, then froze.

Dear God, suppose the damn beach had been sown with mines? He stood still for almost a minute before a sardonic kind of resignation took over. Too damn late now and, if mines were here, he could easily tread on one trying to get back into the water.

He crouched down very carefully and began to change, unpacking the pod at the same time. He began to think about the situation. If there actually were mines, who had put them there? The outside world to stop intruders getting in, or the islanders themselves to keep investigators from getting in?

It seemed an odd situation; when one stopped to think about it, none of it made sense. Hell, he just had to get on with it and he was well equipped. He had small capsules, which converted a flask of sea water into a saltless drink. He had little brown pills which, when dropped into that water, not only provided strong coffee but heated it at the same time. Milk and sugar pills were an added bonus.

He dressed, drank a cup of coffee, and looked at the gun and felt cold inside. One of the new recoil-less Magnums capable of blowing a man in half. Not that such a shot was necessary, with this Magnum one needed only a hit. The impact of the missile induced such a shock to the entire nervous system that death was inevitable.

Peter pushed the weapon into the holster provided, determined not to use it unless his own life was directly threatened.

He turned from the sea to the island, forty or so metres of soft golden sand and then the green of tropical vegetation. Some distance beyond the feathery fronds of palm-like trees rose high above it.

He looked at the jungle again, put on the tele-headband and made adjustments. The mini-camera embedded in the band would now follow the movements of his eyes. If he looked left, the camera would do the same, if he stopped and stared, the camera would stare with him.

He squared his shoulders and trudged up the beach. The soft sand seemed to pull at his feet with every step as if reluctant to let him go.

He pushed his way into the undergrowth but it was not impenetrable, there was no need for the machete with which he had been provided. As he walked on he found there were small pleasant clearings.

Crossing the third, he tripped and fell flat on his face. He got up, swearing. He had fallen heavily, knocked the breath from his body and hurt his ribs. At his age, it was something of a shock to the system and he looked angrily for the cause.

A root, perhaps a large stone hidden in the grass? He could see his foot marks and retraced his steps, nearly tripping again. He stared angrily at the ground, there must be *something*; surely he had not tripped over his own feet twice?

He put his foot forward cautiously and was shocked to see it brought to a halt by *nothing*. He bent down and saw that his toe was almost touching two blades of grass.

He withdrew his foot, went down on his knees and made a cautious exploration with his hands. 'Nothing' rose just above his ankle and was about the length and breadth of his foot. It was not, as he had expected, a solid. It was not like invisible glass or a similar substance—it was repellent. Pushed against, it pushed back. Peter realised his mood had changed from an uneasy apprehension, to something very close to fright. There was something about this place which seemed to pour something icy at the back of his neck and down his spine.

He would need the machete after all, he decided. He needed to probe the ground in front of him and, more important, the area immediately in front. Suppose there was 'nothing' at face level, he could find himself with a black eye or even a broken nose.

Twenty paces on, the machete bounced off a tree. He studied it carefully, the growth appeared perfectly healthy but he was unable to touch. It was as if someone or something had poured this nothing stuff all over. He was unable to touch it, a hand's breadth from the trunk was the nearest he could get to touching it. It was as if the tree was encased in this invisible substance—to what purpose? Nothing here made any sense at all.

Thirty seconds later he saw the wasp.

The wasp was almost in his face and the machete sweep must have missed it completely.

He stepped back quickly, cursing. A painful sting by a tropical insect was something he could do without right now.

It was then that he realised that the wasp hadn't moved. It was still in the air. The wings were not moving, it was fixed, literally, like a fly trapped in amber.

He tried to touch it but half way to it, his hand was once again stopped by something invisible.

Cautious probing with hands and fingers indicated that a sheer wall of nothingness rose in front of him. He looked about him helplessly and, as he did so, other things became apparent.

A brightly coloured tropical bird, wings extended, hung motionless above a palm tree. Three dead leaves were locked unmoving at different heights below a branch. To his left, only a short distance from the wasp was a blur of distortion. Looking closer he saw it was a mass of gnat-like insects, trapped, like everything else in nothingness.

He was not close to panic but he had the certain feeling that his courage was seeping away. Suppose this—whatever it was—was expanding. He, too, might become like the wasp, trapped in invisible amber.

He remembered which way he had come and made his way cautiously back to the beach. Once there he dropped to the sand with an immense sigh of relief.

Is this what had happened to the people on the base, immersed in this dreadful invisible substance? It was only a few hours now, according to the scientists, when the dreadful conditions on the island reverted to normal. When they did so, he was not sure if he wanted to go in and see it. The idea of scores of bodies, rigidly dead, was not something he wanted to see.

What had they been working on? No one had precisely stated the nature of the project, although it was generally supposed it was something to do with space travel. On the other hand it could have been weapon research and this dreadful place mirrored an experiment which had gone wrong.

Peter brushed sweat from his face, looked out across the sea and stiffened—what now?

The blue tropical ocean had only a slight and gentle swell and the air was clear yet there was no mistaking the grey shapes on the far horizon—battle ships. Smaller vessels pulling away from them were also familiar to him, he had seen them in historical films of World War 2—they were landing craft.

He rose, he kicked at the sand angrily with his foot. Nothing made sense anymore, every fragment of information collected was contradicted by another fragment. The entire set-up was a gigantic jig-saw puzzle made up of parts never intended to fit. He wondered briefly if the people on the base had really understood what they were doing when the project had begun in the first year of the New Century unimaginatively called 'The Millennium Project.'

In truth Arthur Calman had understood it very well, too well for peace of mind. He, and his fellow leading scientist, Ernst Hartrein, sat discussing the matter far into the night—many nights. They had become firm friends and both were dedicated scientists.

"Who would have believeda project so innocent could turn up this?"

"Quite so, and let's face it, to such a pointless end. This is a prestige trip, if it ever comes off. There's nothing on Mars, nothing man can bring back for profit or exploitation. No precious minerals, health-giving plants, but just world pride —'look: we have been to Mars.'

Hartrein's mouth thinned visibly. "Not with my help, not with my figures."

"We must thank our lucky stars that we never fed the final

equations into the computer. Without them they can never copy the findings."

Calman poured himself another coffee. "You were the one who saw the danger. In all innocence we have contrived the most dreadful weapon the world has ever seen. Think if it fell into the wrong hands, organised crime could not only strip the world in weeks but enslave the survivors."

"I know, I know." Hartrein nodded quickly. "The point is, what are we going to do about it? Obvious sabotage is out of the question, billions have been sunk into this project. The investors would not only crucify us but everyone on the island."

"I'm well aware of that but I have been thinking about the problem. As you say, any attempt to interfere with the computers is out of the question but how about the generators?"

"A new angle, yes." Hartrein looked hopeful. "What had you in mind?"

"Well, number four is a replacement if you remember, the original had problems from the first. Anyway, said replacement has a minor inspection panel at the far side. I was thinking if some foreign body was introduced when our findings were on the computer screen we could wipe it clean."

"By God, my friend, you've got something. It would also wipe the screens connected to us all over the world. How do you propose to go about this?"

"Something quite simple. I thought about a fly. Foreign body, circuit interference resulting in a brief surge of power."

"Will they suspect?"

"Undoubtedly, but they will never be able to prove."

"Think—figuratively speaking, Mars could have been made in days. I can't help feeling something of a traitor."

"Nor I, but we could never permit such a dreadful weapon to reach the world, let us fix a time—"

* * * * * * * *

The time was fixed for approximately 10 a.m. the following day. It was five minutes late, actually introducing the foreign body had taken longer than expected. When the surge of power came, the computers in the main control room, and in the laboratories, obediently blanked out but outside it was a different story.

A curious spinning cloud of milky luminescence seemed to envelope almost the entire island for a brief period only to vanish in a sharp pink flash.

No one appeared to feel anything and there were no complaints of side effects.

Calman grinned to himself. It had worked, no doubt about that, the brief surge of power had wiped out everything. No need to contact Hartrein, this was his rest day. If, later, the other contacted him that would be normal and not arouse suspicion.

In the meantime he was going down to the beach for a swim.

He never made it. As he approached the shore, four black-clothed and goggled figures rose in his path. All were armed and an amplified voice boomed at him.

"Stand still—raise your hands very slowly and place them on the on the top of your head—go down on your knees—. If you attempt to resist we have orders to shoot."

Rough hands grasped his arms jerking them behind his back, something metallic locked his wrists together. He was searched and jerked upright.

"Stand still, facing that wall, do not attempt to turn—your name?"

"Arthur Calman."

"Sir, to you—I am First Lieutenant Raine."

"You're asking respect after this treatment? Go to hell."

"So they were right, you're a bunch of damned insurgents here."

A voice at a distance said: "The V.I.P launch has just pulled in, Sir."

"V.I.P's! How did they get into the act? I was given to understand this was a military operation."

"An M.P. told me it's Mr. M'Gregor, sir, but I don't know if it's true or not."

"M'Gregor!" A lot of the aggression faded from the Lieutenant's rather hectoring voice. "Get the men in line and to attention, sergeant—*now*, man."

If humanity was due to produce supermen, M'Gregor was the

first but he was not the type so often depicted in fiction. He was not a super intellectual but he was a super personality. He had 'presence,' he radiated power, authority and logical thinking. He had become the confidant of Kings and Presidents and was respected worldwide.

He was a big, craggy man, with a mass of untidy red hair. The blue eyes had the disquieting habit of making many people ill at ease.

He looked the Lieutenant up and down insultingly. "Why in God's name are you garbed out for chemical warfare, Lieutenant?"

"The Commander was not sure of conditions here, sir. He thought it best to be on the safe side as he was worried about his men."

"And where is the Commander?"

"He was called away on urgent business just as we were leaving."

"Ah!"

"Sir?"

"You may interpret that ejaculation in any way you see fit, soldier. In the meantime, get your men out of this ridiculous garb immediately. In this climate they could be suffering from heat stroke in no time at all."

"My orders were, sir—"

The Lieutenant was not permitted to finish the sentence. M'Gregor removed a caller from his pocket. "Shall I call the High Command or would you prefer to do so yourself? This caller has a priority line."

The Lieutenant began to bark orders to his men. His face was pale and he had a chewed look but M'Gregor hadn't finished with him.

"What is this civilian doing here in hand restraints?"

"He was the first one we came across, sir, one of the insurgents. Says his name is Arthur Calman."

M'Gregor gave a start, then glared at the hapless officer.

"Insurgents! What insurgents? Who told you there was insurrection on this island, soldier?"

"Well, sir, there were so many contradictory stories going around that the Commander decided to take no chances."

M'Gregor leaned towards him his face slightly flushed. "Release that man immediately and when you have done so you will apologise, is that clearly understood? An apology does not mean the single word 'sorry.' Unless you wish to face a court martial, you will grovel, bearing in mind that, in the not too distant future I shall be having your Commander's guts for garters. For God's sake, man, start thinking for yourself."

He paused and looked directly at the other. "Yes, I am being hard on you, Lieutenant but to your face and not behind your back. So, to your face, you will instruct your men to say they are here on a security matter, that is, to check the safety of the beaches. They will tell the inhabitants that there is no cause for alarm, that and no more. Under no circumstances are members of your force to say more than that. No passing the time of day or conversations about the mainland – you are following me closely?"

"Yes, sir, most carefully."

"Excellent, now, one final order. I have taken over Room 2 in the Administration Building over there. Kindly put through a request on the area intercom for a Mr. Ernst Hartrein. A request you will note, but an urgent one, thank you."

Hartrein joined Calman five minutes later. "What goes on?"

"I haven't a clue. I know the military are checking the beaches but that is all. They're very tight-lipped, perhaps there's some sort of espionage scare."

"What is that damn great sheet of glass stuck on the wall over there?"

"I know nothing about that either, it was here when I arrived. Oh, yes, one other thing, this whole show is apparently being run by a civilian, a chap called M'Gregor."

M'Gregor entered a few seconds later and introduced himself. "Please make yourselves comfortable gentlemen. Tea, coffee—something stronger?"

He looked at them both thoughtfully. "Please make a selection, I'm afraid this is going to be a very long and trying session for you both."

"Are we on trial or something?" Hartrein looked worried

"On trial? Good heavens, no. I know what you did and why but I am the only one who knows. Frankly I applaud your decision, although others may take a different view, should they find out, but they cannot prove it, can they?"

"You speak as if you knew us intimately," said Calman uneasily.

"Very true."

"Would you mind telling us why you are here?"

"Firstly I am here to find out whether the conclusions I have drawn are correct. Secondly, as gently as possible, to reveal certain uncomfortable truths to you but, bear with me, please, one thing at a time."

He drew a deep audible breath. "You may have noticed that a gentleman has just entered by the side door. He has taken an oath of silence until called upon to speak. Please ignore him for the moment."

M'Gregor paused again and looked penetratingly at both men in turn. "You were sent here, basically, to simplify space travel. Scientific opinion at the time was obsessed with the idea of faster than light travel and subsequent sorties into time/space. My research gives me to understand that the theory could not be married to technology."

"The unit we devised," said Hartrein, "would have been as big as a two story building. Present technology is not quite up to building a space ship round it."

"So you tackled the problem from another angle, that is from the interior of the vessel?"

"Yes." Calman still felt he was somehow on trial. "We tried out the theory on small animals and it appeared successful."

M'Gregor nodded slowly. "It was, at this point, you saw the danger."

"We both saw it," said Calman. "Here was a way to the stars but, at the same time, here also was one of the most dreadful weapons ever devised."

"With it," said Hartrein, taking up the story, "one could have conquered, ravished and bled white an entire nation without it being able to lift a finger to stop you. On a smaller scale—the device could have been miniaturised—crooks could have cleaned out a bank without the staff even knowing."

M'Gregor nodded slowly. "This much I have deduced from

reason but, worse, a man or a group of men could have conquered the world. You did right to take the law into your own hands. I know how it was done, you first destroyed the equations, the pertinent data and all experimental notes. You then contrived a surge of power that would not only wipe clean your computers but all those abroad attuned to them. Gentlemen, many may have their suspicions but none can prove them. By logical argument and circumstantial evidence I could probably bring you before a tribunal but I shall never do that. I can but weep for you, for all of you on this island, for you cannot escape unpunished."

"But I thought you said—" began Calman, angrily.

M'Gregor cut him short. "*Please*, permit me to explain, no trial by men, no punishment by men, but you still have to face the consequences of your actions. To over-simplify, if you puncture a water main beneath the ground in a desperate attempt to seal a dangerous gas leak, you will still have to deal with flooding however successful your attempts to avert disaster may have been."

"What are you trying to tell us?" Hartrein had a premonition of imminent disaster.

"I have a great deal to tell you, but, please, permit me to explain it, gently, in my own way, without interruptions. To begin with, name a city, any city."

Calman scowled at him, still angry. "What the hell, why not something way out, like The City of Angels."

"Los Angeles, certainly." M'Gregor made a curious gesture with his hand and the object which the two men had assumed to be a huge sheet of glass swirled briefly with rainbows. Then they were looking down on a sunlit city from a medium height.

Los Angeles, both men recognised it and were shocked by the clearness of the picture and the advanced type of screen.

"Taking you down to look at the traffic." M'Gregor made another gesture. "The screen responds to simple hand signals," he explained, "although the new ones respond to spoken commands—look at the traffic."

They looked and both men felt a coldness envelop them. The highway was even more crowded then they remembered but all the vehicles were of a different shape. All appeared virtually silent and many of the cars were wheel-less.

"Note, no smog," said M'Gregor. "All traffic operates from beamed power. The internal combustion engine is only employed in those back of beyond places where distributor towers have yet to be erected."

Calman swallowed audibly. "I know I'm stating the obvious but you're from the future, aren't you?"

"Relatively speaking, that is true."

"We don't understand you."

"This is our *present* but it is *your future*."

"We don't follow." Both men were aware of a growing apprehension.

"I am trying to spell this out as gently and as lucidly as possible," M'Gregor's voice was both compassionate and compelling. "Consider, please, a warm, gentle stream running through the countryside. We can, employing certain technologies, cause a block of ice to occur in the middle of that stream. The warm waters flow past it but the ice remains, please keep that simile in mind."

He paused and looked at the two men intently. "I know about the Mars Project but I should be grateful if you would explain the means you hoped to use. At this moment such a point may appear irrelevant but believe me, it will help us all."

Hartrein, his face pale, answered first. "Well, as we told you, we had to dump our first theory, it was too big to get off the ground. Still working on the time/space theory we stumbled on a new factor."

Hartrein stopped. "Calman can explain this part better than I."

"Only in a simplified way." Calman was cold inside but soaked in perspiration and not quite sure why. "We found that by the application of certain electrical counter forces on various wavelength and frequencies, we could effect the passage of time. We set about constructing such a unit to fit into a space ship."

Hartrein took up the theme again. "The idea being this, your space vessel would still take years or months to make its journey, but within the vessel time would be virtually frozen. For the crew, transfer would be almost immediate. The time mechanism would switch off as soon as the vessel went into orbit round Mars. The process would be repeated for return to Earth. It was at this point we both realised how our discovery could be converted into the most terrible weapon mankind had ever devised."

"True, very true." M'Gregor nodded slowly. "We realised that, or at least a small number of us. We deliberately leaked many untrue stories about this island in order to keep the curious away. Some very special observers were sent in but there was only one clear approach and long range cameras took this picture."

He made a gesture and the screen lit again. "The tennis courts. You recognise the players perhaps?"

"Why, yes." Calman leaned forward. "Maria Frassetti, playing Leonard Peel—is it important?"

"The players are not, the picture is. Note that Mr. Peel's left foot is not touching the ground as he reaches for the ball. Note the gull overhead and the palm leaf falling in the corner of the picture. Here is a second, a third, a fourth and the final fifth. What do you see, gentlemen?"

"They're all the damn same." Hartrein's voice was a croak. "That is true in every detail—they were taken at ten year intervals." He waved them quickly to silence before they could ask questions. "Tell me, what was the common denominator of your calculations?"

"Fifty." Calman almost choked on the word, everything was falling horribly into place.

"On what day and at what hour did you delete the data?"

"Around ten in the morning, April 23rd, the year 2000."

"In short, today?"

"Well, yes. It is now—" He stopped, almost aware of the answer.

M'Gregor looked away and when he spoke his voice was very gentle. "Today *this day*, is April 23rd and the year is *Two thousand and fifty*."

Hartrein was no longer listening, he felt as if a huge wound had been opened up inside him. Vanda with her soft body and hungry lips, they would have been married in June. Vanda, if she had survived the years, would be eighty-one now, white-haired, perhaps walking with a stick.

It was as bad for Calman also but it was going to worsen as the minutes passed. He had had a six-week-old son on the mainland, but now…?

M'Gregor made a gesture to the man who had come in late. "Will you join us now, please?"

Calman saw him and didn't see him. A tall man, thin, greying, face worldly wise and lined. He seemed vaguely familiar. What the hell did he have to do with them?

M'Gregor resumed his theme. "Your device should have had a safety casing. When wrecked the computers released a time-freezing energy that effected a greater part of the island. As the basic denominator was fifty, time was frozen in that year for that number of years. You were the ice in the stream, fixed, while normal time flowed past you."

They stared at him, understanding but not wanting to understand. Almost they hated him, changing everything, killing their lives with words.

"We picked up a reporter earlier," continued M'Gregor. "He found time rather like ice—a solid thing. He was unable to pass through it because one cannot walk into the past."

He paused again and looked directly into Calman's young strained face. "There is no way I can tell you this with kindness, sir –I'm sorry. This reporter, this man I have just called down to join us—this is your son Peter."

Sometimes they line the shore and stare across the ocean. They are free to leave but none try. The twenty-year old father stands beside his fifty-year old son knowing that here is gulf which can never be bridged.

PLAYTHING

by Ken Alden

Kenwood had so much excited energy that he clapped his hands together as he walked along.

"Looks like our sort of place don't you think?" he announced with great pleasure.

I gave the world a quick look over as I hurried along behind him. It was all cheap, ugly huts and even uglier aliens. It certainly wasn't the sort of place I wanted to be associated with.

"Say, maybe we can find a bitch for you," he babbled on, pleased with himself. "You know what I mean, blue eyes, blond hair, fangs."

"No thank you," I politely told him. "I'm keeping myself pure."

The grin got bigger. "Oh yeah."

"Yes."

Ever since my death I had avoided bitches. They were a temptation I could do without.

"You can smell money can't you?" Kenwood went on.

"I suppose so," I agreed.

Actually I could smell quite a few nasty things and money was not one of them.

"Come on, lighten up will you."

I gave his back a good glare. Kenwood is that most irritating of things, the class-mate who has done better than you. He lets you know it as well with his expensive suits, flashy vehicles, the best hair money can buy, the best food, the best this, the best that, and it is all topped off with that sort of happy cockiness that goes right up your nose.

"Come on minion, let's have some smiles out of you," he demanded without even looking in my direction.

And believe me, if there is anything more irritating than an old class-mate who has done good, it is one who is employing you.

"Come on, smile," he repeated. "When you are strolling into a camp packed to overflowing with blood-thirsty mass murderers you've got to look friendly."

"My face doesn't work that way," I told him.

Ahead of us now were the barracks. These consisted of a concrete defence wall and, beyond that, some flat roofed, single storey concrete buildings. Delicate architects would probably throw up at the sight of it all.

"Tell rat face to let us through then," Kenwood told me as we neared the gate.

I, you see, am a translator.

"This is Tim Kenwood," I dutifully told the guard. "We are here to see Lord Timor."

The guard looked us up and down. It was *Nrentor,* the prominent race around here. That meant it was basically humanoid in shape but that peeking out of its elaborate armour was a face which, to real humans, looked like that of a six foot high rat. All of which will give you a clue as to their personality.

The thing squeaked aggressively at me.

"It wants your ID card," I told Kenwood.

"Yeah. I guessed the sweet little darling would."

He pulled out the card, and it was pushed into the gateway's computer terminal.

And just as the guard did this, my nose began to tingle. I could smell dog.

I took a few steps forward so that I could stare into the barracks. There it was. A large guard dog had just jumped up onto a wall in order to stare at me.

"Scram," I said to it, and to emphasize the point I growled at it with my original set of vocal cords.

The animal's eyes widened with alarm. It took two steps backwards. Then with a forlorn yelp, it abruptly disappeared from sight.

It could sense that there was something the matter with me all right.

The computer buzzed contentedly away to itself for a minute or so more as it checked the DNA record on the card with what it could sense in Kenwood's body. Satisfied, it spat the card out.

Instinctively I jumped up and caught it in my mouth.

"Good boy." Kenwood patted me on the head.

"Get de' ad off," I attempted to mumble.

I spat out the card myself. For about half a second I planned to sink my fangs into the patronizing bastard. He couldn't treat me in that condescending way. Then the human side of me regained control and the canine anger was suppressed.

Kenwood strolled on into the barracks, unaware of how close he had come to being savaged.

"Down, boy," I muttered.

It was two years since they switched bodies on me, and I still hadn't got full control of this one. I picked up the card in my mouth and padded after Kenwood.

You see when my battleship was blasted apart there had been nearly two thousand corpses floating out there in space, all of them loudly demanding immediate replacement. The medics soon ran out of monkey bodies, so when they extracted my brain patterns they had to go and impose them on those of a dog.

"Consider yourself lucky," my Death Counsellor told me when I whined about this. "Not all soldiers appreciate being turned into monkeys. They might even have had pigs in stock."

"Come on, don't dawdle!" Kenwood yelled back at me.

I padded after him, my grip on the ID card getting tighter. His smell was getting stronger I noticed. That had to mean our contact was close.

We passed a few ugly buildings, found a parade ground and, yes, there he was. Sitting on a bench beside this ground was Kenwood—the original Kenwood.

"You boys took your time didn't you?"

He got up and strolled towards us. He managed to have a strut that was even cockier than the Duplicate's. He also had one of those small black cigars in his mouth. As he spoke, the cigar wiggled about, and for some reason this offended my delicate sensibilities, not to mention my equally delicate nose. I did a bit of frustrated teeth clenching as well. This rich bastard could afford to have his consciousness duplicated and transferred to a fast-grown clone, while I could only afford to have mine transferred to a mangy mutt.

"Ah, there's a handsome looking fellow."

The original went and patted the Duplicate on the cheek.

"Handsome and rich," added the clone as he tickled the original under the chin. And having got all that out they both had a boisterous laugh at each other.

"Let's have that." The Duplicate snatched the card from my mouth. He fingered its touch patches. "It's my DNA. We're alright." He winked at himself. "You aren't here, boy."

"You could have fooled me."

The original jerked his head over his shoulder in an attempt to indicate a particularly large eyesore.

"That's where we are heading."

"Right."

So we headed for it. And I would like to make it clear—just in case this manuscript falls into the hands of the authorities—that I padded along behind the others with great reluctance. I, for one, wasn't keen to help blood-thirsty mass murderers.

As we neared the building we heard a few noises that could have been an attempt at singing, and if it was singing it was the sort of a tune you only attempt after several pints of something illegal.

A figure stepped out of the building to greet us. For a second I thought it might be some pompous old-world major-domo. It had that sort of uniform. Only the metal face did not fit.

"Good day sir," this robot said to us in English, and it gave a little bow.

"Take us to your leader, tin man," Kenwood called out in an extra loud voice. He then exchanged a grin with himself just to make sure his other half appreciated his own wit.

"'Do you mean Lord Timor sir?" the robot inquired.

"That's the man, boy."

"Ah, very good sir. We have been waiting for you. Kindly step this way."

It led us into the building and along a corridor. The singing got louder.

"I don't know if you are aware sir," said the robot, "but Lord Timor's English is rather limited."

"Yeah, well, so's mine," Kenwood said. "Usually limit it to four letter words, I do."

He exchanged another grin with himself.

"I might be able to help you, however, sir," the robot continued in its slow, cultivated, upper class tones. "I have been programmed to translate several languages—"

"We can translate for ourselves," I told it in rough *Nrentor.*

"Very good sir. I did not appreciate that fact." The top half of the robot swivelled round so that it could give me a little bow while the legs kept on marching forward.

"In fact your presence won't be required during the negotiations," I added in the same language. We didn't want our plans upset by people who knew what was going on.

"Very well, if you wish sir," the robot said with its irritating politeness. There wasn't even the hint of irony you would expect from a human butler.

The singing reached a crescendo just as we entered the barrack's mess. The principal tenor then fell over onto his face, and all that the rest of the choir could manage was some indistinct mumbling.

"What name shall I give?" the major-domo asked.

And I must admit that it was a question that, for a moment, floored me. It also clearly floored both our Kenwoods. People like them have at least a dozen names, many of them not usable in polite society.

"What?" one of them asked.

"What name shall I give?" he repeated. "I have to announce you."

"Oh, Fred Bloggs," said the other. "Fred Bloggs and friend." He glanced at me. "And pet."

I let out a canine growl.

"And you can stop making that sort of noise," said a Kenwood as he pointed a finger at me.

I switched back to my mechanical vocal cords. "It's John Smith," I lied to the major-domo.

But the robot was already preparing to announce us. His nose had gone up in the air and his manner had got a bit more pompous.

"Mr. Fred Bloggs, friend and pet," he bellowed.

The two Kenwoods sauntered into the mess. A couple of people stared, empty eyed, at them and that was about it as far as greetings went.

"It's John Smith," I snarled at the robot.

"I do apologize sir. I did not mean to give offence."

The nose went up. "Mr. John Smith," he announced.

"Thank you."

I padded forward.

Most of the creatures in the room were warriors. You could tell they were warriors because there was so much spiked armour, and so many horned helmets and assorted weapons scattered around. The advanced drunkenness and general ugliness of everyone present was another clue.

The robot joined the Kenwoods and me.

"I will inform Lord Timor of your presence," he said before walkinstiffly off to somewhere or other.

A particularly big warrior staggered towards us. It was another rat-faced Nrentor.

"Urm wresl ur for ten cred," it said.

And the thing was waving its arms around in what I believe was an attempt to flex its sizeable muscles.

"Come again friend?" a Kenwood asked.

"Arm wrestle yha for ten credits," it repeated. Both the Kenwoods grinned.

"No thanks, friend. You're too big and strong for us," said one.

"Ummmm?" The Nrentor creased its brow in puzzlement and swayed about as it took this in.

"Perhaps another time," added the other.

The warrior grabbed a bottle from a table and waved it about. "Damn mechanical," he told us, and he threw the bottle at the door the robot had just exited through.

He then realized, to his horror, what he had done. He stared with alarm at the empty paw and then transferred the alarmed gaze to the remains of the bottle.

"Mur ger dumb," he said.

After which he took two steps towards the remains and fell over.

So this, I told myself, was the feared Vorotor. Here we had the warriors who planted bombs and then demanded protection money. Here were the monsters who massacred millions, or at least tens of thousands, or maybe it was a few hundred for all I knew. Whatever the figure was it was too big.

I had to show my attitude to these fearless warriors, so I went over to the nearest unconscious example and cocked my leg.

"Lord Timor, the almighty leader," the robot announced.

And his Lordship marched into the room with a kingly stride. I won't say that he was sober, but at least he could manage a straight line. He made straight for us anyway.

I had been expecting a *Nrentor*. He was instead, however, an armour-covered *Terner*. That meant he was another six foot tall humanoid. Though the eyes were far apart, the face was lumpy, the skin was scaly and there were a lot of running sores.

The original Kenwood stepped forward.

"Ah, your Lordship, I am so pleased to be in your presence."

He gave a little nod which, I guess, was his attempt at a bow. He also came up with that ingratiating salesman's smile of his.

I translated his greeting.

His Lordship waved it aside. He, presumably, didn't want all the salesman stuff. We had the blunt, forthright warrior sort here.

"How much do you want for your weapons?" he demanded.

"Forty thousand," I said; because I had been authorized to negotiate.

"Thirty."

"Thirty eight."

"Thirty three."

"Thirty five."

"Thirty four."

That was the price we had earlier agreed on, so I passed the news on to Kenwood.

"Done," he said.

And that was it. We had travelled endless light years, created a clone to confuse the identification machine, put ourselves in considerable danger and it was all sorted out within a few breaths. We had agreed to break umpteen laws and supply arms to some of the nastiest terrorists going.

Altogether I felt a strong desire to puke up my vegetarian dog biscuits.

Control it, I told myself as I tried to push these thoughts aside. I couldn't let the canine anger take over too often. If you do that the dog can regain control. Brilliant people have ended up barking mad and scratching for fleas.

"Tell him about the plaything," Kenwood told me.

So I did. "We will also be providing humans for your amusement," I said. "Just as we agreed." And you should have seen the way he brightened up at this news.

"How many?" he demanded.

"Oh, a number," I said. Nobody had given me any figures.

"And what sort?"

"Oh, all sorts."

"Good, good." He grinned and nodded away, evidently pleased with our bribe.

"He likes that idea does he?" asked my equally pleased employer.

"It looks like it," I coldly told him.

"I thought he would. Bastard's got a collection you know."

"Has he?" I said. "And where were you thinking of getting these human additions to it? The Job Centre?"

Kenwood rolled his little cigar around in his grinning mouth. "Oh, we are reorganising the firm's administrative section."

"Are we indeed," I said.

And I must say it all seemed to fit. Here was your typical employer: eager to sell his employees for the amusement of aliens. Eager to lord it and buy wildly over-priced items while you worry yourself sick about money, eager to put you down, pat your head, call you pet, and generally bully you just as he did at school.

However, as all these thoughts passed through my head they were followed by a rather brilliant, if nasty, idea.

That's it, I mentally told myself, and, no doubt, for the first time in history a dog smiled. I had just worked out how to pull off the last part of our plan.

"You can have your first plaything now if you like," I said to Lord Timor.

"I can?"

His eyes darted around, presumably searching for this toy.

"It's here," I said, gesturing at my old school mate.

And Kenwood, who, of course, did not have a clue what I was saying, smiled.

"It's a clone of him," I said.

Lord Timor's puzzled gaze turned from me to Kenwood then back to me.

"He sent a copy of himself?" he asked.

You could tell he did not believe it, and I have got to admit that this was probably because it was not very believable.

"He has strange tastes," I explained.

Lord Timor's gaze became less puzzled and moved up and down Kenwood.

"Well, in that case I will take him."

I switched languages.

"He wants to show you his personal den," I told Kenwood. "It's a great privilege apparently, so only you can see it – very private place, it seems."

Kenwood let out a snort of a laugh. That smug, self-satisfied grin of his got even more irritating.

"Well now, that sounds my sort of thing. Tell him I'll be very pleased to see it."

I switched again.

"You might find this one struggles and protests a lot, but that is all part of the game." I winked at the scaly killer. "You know how humans like to play games."

Lord Timor winked back.

"Oh yes, I've heard of that."

"You'd better take him there, now."

And so this fiend in almost human shape smiled at my employer, and my employer smiled back at the fiend. Lord Timor then took Kenwood by the arm and led him off to a dark corridor.

"Did you get all that?" I asked the Duplicate.

The Duplicate licked his front tooth. The recorder hidden in it played back the most incriminating part of Kenwood's conversation.

"Right, it was you that said that," I told him.

The Duplicate became alarmed. "It was?"

"There has been a slight change of plan. Only you came here."

"Yes, but—"

"That ID card will prove it, remember."

"But—"

"You and I were working together in order to gain proof that Kenwood's firm was sanctions busting. That's why you came here and imitated him. Kenwood got wind of it, though, realized the game was up and ran. Nobody knows where he is, but we still managed to destroy his firm and stop the arms shipments."

"Are you going to explain all this to me in simple terms?" the Duplicate asked.

"Later, let's get out of here first."

"One moment if you will, sir." The robot came hurrying up to us. "His Lordship has asked me to make an inquiry."

"Oh yes?" I said.

"He isn't that sure what you do with humans. He was asking if you could show him."

"Oh, tell him to experiment. He will find a way eventually. Now if you will excuse us we have a 'bus to catch."

And I leapt up, put my front paws on Kenwood's back and pushed him out of there as fast as I could.

Why aliens find humans sexually attractive I have no idea. I mean, would you want to go to bed with a three eyed scaly thing? Of course not, so why should the scaly thing want to go to bed with you? But for some reason it seems us humans have got "it"...

A MATTER OF VIBRATION

by Sydney J. Bounds and John Russell Fearn

Will Gregory was alone in his laboratory when the manifestations began.

He often worked late after the day's routine, puzzling over the few papers left by his father, and his reconstruction of the molecular vibrator. He was determined to find out just where David Gregory's experiment had gone wrong.

His father had believed that electrons did not so much exist as concrete things, but as probabilities, as liable to be shifted out of their positions in space-time as a mist was dispersed by a breeze. Nothing *was*: all that existed was the *probability* of its existence.

He sat at his workbench before a visual display unit, watching a column of numbers change as the computer worked through his latest theory.

"Obviously something to do with molecular structure," he murmured. "And vibration. What the devil was he after, I wonder?"

He became aware of eyes watching him, eyes set in a grey mask. A face had appeared in the VDU screen, faint and shadowy behind the numbers. He blinked, and the face faded away.

"Didn't think I was that tired—imagining faces now!"

Then he sensed movement off to one side, and jerked around. He saw nobody. He was alone in the brightly-lit physics lab.

He was turning back to the screen when the door silently opened. Will waited but nobody came in. He left his chair, crossed the room and looked down an empty corridor.

"Anyone there?" he called. There was no answer.

He closed the door and returned to his seat, mildly uneasy—then jumped in surprise as his father's papers rose into the air and hovered there as if held by an invisible hand.

"Must be a draught—can't be anything else."

The papers settled back on his workbench, but in a different order. One paragraph of the topmost paper glowed with a strange light and he read it through:

If electrons exist only as probabilities, as Heisenberg theorised, the right vibration should cause a shift in molecular structure. This shift could perhaps be the gateway to another dimension, not by actual physical transportation, but by the altered molecules vibrating in sympathy with another plane of matter.

He'd read his father's words many times before but now, as the glow faded, they assumed greater importance.

He looked up, frowning. There was a draught coming from somewhere, but the door and windows were closed. But, damn it, there was a draught, and a cold one for such a mild evening in early Autumn.

He put on his coat and glanced at a thermometer on the wall; the mercury had fallen to freezing point. Impossible! Temperature didn't drop that fast.

He switched on a heater and looked out of a window. People were strolling casually along the road, without overcoats. Strange.

He got on with his work but began to feel alarmed as a cloud of biting cold enveloped him. "What the hell's happening?"

Then the numbers on his computer screen vanished and words mysteriously replaced them:

WILL, IT'S ME, VERA.

He stared at the screen, and shivered as the words changed.

I WANT TO GET BACK, WILL. HELP ME.

He typed:

IS THIS SOME SORT OF JOKE?

WHO ARE YOU?

His words were wiped out:

NOT JOKING, WILL. IT'S ME, VERA MORTON.

Will felt his scalp tighten. "Vera Morton?" He had difficulty speaking the name: it brought back a painful memory. "Why, that was years ago…"

* * * * * * * *

He'd only been eight when the explosion happened. Vera Morton, aged six, had been his best friend and always said his father's lab was a scary place, but she trusted him,

They should never have been in the laboratory in the first place, but the night security guard knew Will by sight—and he was the boss's son.

Young Will, excited, held Vera's small hand and led her along a corridor. Quietly he opened the door of the lab and looked inside. He was too young to understand everything he saw; thick cables, a high-tension terminal and the molecular vibrator.

His father was bending over a test-bench, absorbed in an ever-changing list of numbers on-screen; his finger rested on a push-button. There was a smell of ozone and the air almost crackled with electricity. The lighting was unusually bright. The room seemed to shake with vibration.

"Quiet," whispered Will. "We mustn't interrupt—just watch."

Vera had been attracted to a calendar on the wall, which had a picture of gaily-plumed birds, and silently edged towards it. So she and Will were separated when his father pushed the button.

A pressure wave surged through the air. The lights brightened and went out. The darkness exploded in flame and David Gregory was hurled through a window, killing him instantly. Will was swept off his feet and slammed senseless against a wall.

The whole building rocked.

The security guard outside picked himself up off the ground, telephoned for an ambulance, and Will was rushed to hospital. Police and fireman searched the building, but there was no sign of Vera. She had vanished, leaving no clue to where she had gone or how she had disappeared. Will was deeply upset when he recovered.

The years passed, and the mystery of Vera Morton's disappearance was forgotten .

* * * * * * * *

Now he was overwhelmed by guilt as he stared at the screen.

I'M SO COLD, WILL.

If he hadn't taken her to his father's laboratory—but he

couldn't have imagined what would happen. He'd been too young then. He shouldn't feel guilty, but he did.

He struggled to understand as frost formed and covered the computer.

I'M STUCK HERE, WILL, AND EVERYTHING'S SO STRANGE.

I'M SCARED. PLEASE HELP ME.

WHERE'S HERE? he tapped out.

I DON'T KNOW. I JUST WANT TO GET HOME.

This wasn't a dream or hallucination, Will Gregory realised. His father's experiment had done this to her and, again, he felt a wave of guilt.

His fingers moved quickly over the keyboard:

ANY EXPERIMENT CAN BE REVERSED, VERA. I'LL GET YOU BACK, I PROMISE.

His numbers reappeared on the screen. He looked at the .big molecular vibrator he had built to his father's specification; there was a flaw somewhere and he had to find it. He had to understand exactly what David Gregory had done and reverse the effect.

He remembered how, at twenty-five, after graduating from Cambridge with a degree in physics, he'd taken over his father's rebuilt laboratory at Normansfield. The few papers that had survived left him puzzled about the nature of David's last experiment. Now it was vital he solve the mystery in a hurry.

He worked on, feeling he was getting somewhere, when—

An icy draught blew around him and he looked sharply at the computer screen.

HURRY, WILL! IT'S SO COLD.

I ALMOST BROKE THROUGH. ALMOST.

CAN YOU SEE ANYTHING?

He sat down at the keyboard and tapped out:

SEE WHAT?

His words were wiped from the screen to leave a blank greyness. Gradually a picture emerged of a bleak landscape of bare rock and ice, with leafless trees, like rotting stumps, sticking up from banks of deep snow.

Slow-moving figures, like empty shrouds, drifted through a swirling mist. There were other shapes that reminded him of wolves; big brutes with savage expressions, hungry and hunting.

Will had never seen anywhere so desolate and felt a shudder ripple along his spine as he thought of Vera. He was frightened for her; how could anyone live in that dreadful place?

He saw no flowers, no colour, anywhere; just shades of grey as if viewed by moonlight. Flurries of snow blew around rocky crags.

Some of the figures might once have been human, coming and going like phantoms, grey and wraithlike. He felt unnerved and, for a moment, even considered shutting down the experiment.

But he couldn't abandon Vera. She fascinated him; what else had she seen in that other dimension? How had she survived? Her experience, if he could get her back, would be unique.

And then, looming through the mist, he saw a face in close-up. Vera! He recognised her dark curls, but now her chubby face had changed and shone with a cold beauty. He was appalled by the knowledge that his father had trapped her in that freezing wasteland.

I SEE YOU, VERA.

She reminded him of a ghost film he had once seen on television. Perhaps, sometimes, a part of this other world touched ours and leaked through. There were tales of apparitions and always they were linked with the idea of coldness. Was this where the notion of ghosts had come from? This limbo between dimensions where some unfortunates ended their lives.

Momentarily, a flickering shadowy figure appeared behind Vera. The figure seemed to be surrounded by strange oscillating lights. Will blinked at the shimmering image, and when he opened his eyes the figure was gone.

Will recalled that he had read accounts of people who disappeared suddenly; there had been many reports of such incidents down the ages. He imagined all these people trapped in that frigid no-man's land.

WILL, SAVE ME.

I'LL GET YOU BACK SOMEHOW, VERA—

I SWEAR I WILL.

The temperature in the laboratory continued to fall, but the computer again showed his equations. He worked on, sure now it was a question of generating a particular kind of vibration; one that changed the molecular structure of matter. His father hadn't got it quite right and his experiment had blown up.

As a physicist, Will knew that the faster molecules moved, the hotter a body became; and the slower the colder. Somehow the molecules making up Vera's body had been slowed down.

The probability that she existed in a plane of matter in a world of humans had yielded abruptly to the probability that she existed in another plane of matter contiguous to Will's own. Could there be intelligent life there? He remembered the shadowy figure on the screen behind Vera, and frowned. How was Vera managing to communicate through his computer?

Perhaps an other-world scientist had discovered how to transmit and receive electronic messages across the dimensional gulf, and was helping Vera try and get back. If there were still a residual rift in the fabric of space here in his laboratory, where the original explosion had occurred, it would explain how Vera had been able to locate, and contact him.

Mystery upon mystery, utter and profound. Their solutions would have to wait whilst Will forced himself to concentrate on the immediate problems.

He studied the results his computer had produced, and thought: I'm going to need more power.

He was doubling up cables to take the extra load when he realised his fingers were numb and his hands turning blue. He stamped his feet and swung his arms vigorously. The windows had frosted over and the thermometer registered a temperature well below zero.

Vera, in trying to get back, had opened up the gap between worlds and a freezing wind blew through.

He rubbed at a window and peered out. With a shock he saw a road like a sheet of ice in the dawn light; most of the night had passed. A few people, well wrapped up in overcoats, scarves and gloves, were making their way to work.

He had never felt so cold and knew he must have a hot drink to keep going. He switched on an electric kettle to make a cup of tea. He glanced at the clock; almost six. While he was waiting for the tea to brew, he turned on his portable radio in time to hear a news bulletin:

"... and this morning," an announcer said, "one part of the country is having freak weather. A severe cold spell, with near-arctic conditions, has dislocated traffic around Normansfield. Canals and reservoirs are frozen over. The rest of the country is enjoying comparatively mild weather, and the forecasters are unable to explain this unusual weather pattern."

Will switched off and drank his tea as ice formed in the lab.

He knew he didn't have much time; Vera's world was now resonating with his own. His hands felt as if they'd been dipped in liquid nitrogen.

A disembodied voice came out of the air: "Will! Will, I'm halfway through. Help me..."

He worked as fast se he could with fumbling fingers.

Then, from the crack between dimensions, a damp mist swirled. Wraithlike forms flitted around him; an icy hand stroked his cheek, leaving behind a smell like an open grave. The air was so cold he could see his breath, puffing like steam from an old locomotive.

A piece of lab equipment was hurled through the air and crashed against a wall. The VDU screen was blank and silent but a howling wind filled the room, mingling with an awful moaning and wailing. Will felt the hairs lift on the back of his neck.

The strange life-forms from beyond seemed to be drawing energy from him and he felt himself weakening. His stomach churned and his skin grew clammy. He'd never been so frightened in his life.

The heavy cable rippled like a snake. He heard a snuffling sound, then a flapping noise as something flew over his head. Greenish eyes glowed in the mist, watching him.

Eventually, he had everything set up the way he wanted.

"Switching on," he said. "Any moment now, Vera, and I'll have you back."

He pressed a button and power surged through the new circuits he had wired up. The molecular vibrator shuddered as he stepped up the power; its sound reached such a high pitch he gritted his teeth. Then it was beyond his range of hearing, but the air pulsated with its vibrations.

Now!

A female body came tumbling out of the air. Vera, looking

younger than he expected; perhaps sixteen, with everything to live for. Will's thoughts raced: slowing molecules of matter must also slow the passage of time.

She was smiling as she got to her feet. "Will! Thank you, Will..."

Then her frozen body, preserved for years, shattered like glass. The wind died and, as the room began to warm up, she shrivelled before his eyes, screaming and calling his name.

But there was nothing he could do. He watched, helpless, as she melted and a pool of evil-smelling and discoloured water spread across the floor of the laboratory, like an oil slick.

Will Gregory covered his face with frost-bitten hands as tears filled his eyes.

DERELICT

by David Somers

Bertha listened to the smooth humming of the engine, tapped readings into the computer log and inserted in the comments column: Optimum. If only she could say the same of the human aspect to this test flight. If only the pilot weren't so macho-minded.

She left the engineering section and stepped into the command area. Dean had Rohini backed into a corner and the young woman was giggling; she didn't seem to realise how serious he was.

Bertha said sharply, "Cut that out, Dean. Get back to your seat and let Rohini get on with her work."

"Keep out of this," he snapped. "You're only jealous because you're too old for fun and games."

Bertha moved forward in a wrestler's crouch. Dean held up his hands in front of his face, mocking. "Spoil these and who'll run the ship?"

"Get back to your station," she said.

Dean slid into his seat at the pilot's console, and Bertha relaxed. Rohini stepped into her lab compartment and bent over her equipment.

Bertha watched Dean watching Rohini, his sensitive fingertips stroking control pads. She imagined those fingers stroking bare skin—Rohini's light brown skin—and thought, why should she care?

Only because the three of them were the entire crew of Earth's first interstellar ship, *Goliath*, travelling at an appreciable fraction of the speed of light and now beyond the rim of the solar system.

Bertha admitted, reluctantly, that Dean had a point. Rohini was slender, her coverall fitted like a body-stocking, and she moved with the ease of someone trained in the ballet. A delicate perfume made both of them acutely aware of her. Could Rohini be as innocent as she appeared? She had recently graduated in theoretical physics and seemed to have her head in another dimension, concerned only with exotic equations.

It was her experiment they were running; an attempt to detect gravity waves with equipment she had designed.

Dean was acknowledged the project's best pilot-astrogator. Closer to Rohini's age, he affected sideburns and a swagger and wore his coverall open to show the hairs on his chest. Some bureaucrat had made an error assigning him a place with two crew-women. Bertha would have been happy with the second best pilot.

It was not really her problem; as the project engineer who knew most about the ship's engine, she had only to check its performance. But too old? Nonsense, she was only forty something; it was her greying hair and muscular body that fooled people. Still, she wanted to get back without incident; she might get to be engineer on the first flight to the nearest star. And it was important to Rohini to carry her experiment through to a conclusion.

The radar went: *ping!* Something out there in the interstellar gulf?

Rohini stopped fussing with her test set-up and moved to stand in front of the screen. Bertha joined her. Dean's fingertips glided over touch-pads, bringing up a picture and sharpening it.

"That looks like a ship!" Rohini gave a gasp of excitement.

Bertha studied the image, feeling uneasy. It was a big ship and not of a design she could recognise. Apparently it was drifting with nobody at the controls.

Dean was cutting speed, juggling to pass close to it. A derelict, with holes in its metal hull; small round holes mostly with no discernible pattern. There was no indication of life aboard.

Dean said tersely, "That wasn't built on Earth."

"We ought to investigate," Rohini said.

It had to be their decision. Even though Dean was talking into a mike and broadcasting to Earth Orbital Station, waiting for a reply was out of the question.

"I vote we board her," he said, and Rohini clapped her

hands. “Oh, yes!”

Bertha had to agree. Obviously an extraterrestrial vessel must be inspected at close quarters and a report sent back to E.O.S.

In the time it took to bring *Goliath* alongside and match speed, Bertha prepared a hot meal. They ate in front of the screen as Dean stroked sensi-pads and watched the derelict grow as he edged closer.

“That’s it,” he said finally. “As near as I’m getting to a thing that size. You’re the engine expert, Bertha. Suit up and take a look at what they use to move it.”

“Leaving you here with Rohini, I suppose? Not likely.”

“I can’t go,” he said. “If anything happened to me, you’d never get back.”

“But I want to go,” Rohini said. “I want to take a look at those holes in the hull.”

Bertha nodded. She didn’t fancy going alone into an alien ship, even if it did seem unoccupied.

Dean opened a locker and handed to her a small electronic device with a suction pad attached and showed her where to switch on. “A tracer.”

“Why?”

“Because whoever follows us out here will want to know where to find it. This wreck’s drifting, and the fixed stars aren’t really fixed. Plotting a position relative to Earth orbit isn’t easy.”

Bertha and Rohini checked each other’s suits. Bertha carried a camera and Rohini a radiation counter.

“One hour,” Dean said. “Any longer I treat as an emergency. Stay in touch.”

Waiting in an open airlock, Bertha studied the exterior of the alien ship. The lock was obvious; it projected from the hull and. beside it, was a mechanical ratchet. In case of power failure, she thought.

She pushed off and floated across the gap. The ratchet was stiff but, finally, she was able to anchor herself and work it free. The lock slowly opened.

“Okay, Rohini, just a gentle push.”

The young woman floated across and Bertha caught her gloved hand and pulled her inside. The inner door was open and Bertha moved into the ship. The corridor was dark and silent, obviously airless; inscribed signs in an unknown language intrigued her. She switched on the headlamp in her suit and photographed them.

"Wait," Rohini said. She checked the first hole she came to with her Geiger. "Some residual radiation."

"So?"

"I'll check others—I've an idea of what might have happened here."

"So long as it doesn't happen to us."

"If I'm right, it could."

Further along the corridor a body sprawled. It was bipedal with a broad thorax, the skin corrugated and leathery. One talon clutched a limp curled up pad.

"Looks like a sticky patch for sealing holes," Bertha said. "Too little and too late." For Dean's information, she reported: "This body looks like it died centuries ago. This ship could have come a long way."

She photographed the corpse and moved on. Rohini checked each hole they passed. The sizes varied but each was round, the sort of hole a missile might make. She didn't look happy with her radiation readings.

"Thirty minutes gone," Dean said.

Bertha pushed ahead till she found the main engine room. There was another body here and a film of dust. She stared, baffled, at massive tubes coiled about a crystalline grid, and spheres pierced by vertical rods.

The only things she recognised were the holes. Whatever had penetrated the hull had also perforated the engine. It remained silent and without power. Bertha clicked her camera.

Dean said, "Time's up. Plant the tracer and return."

"We're coming now," Rohini replied, as Bertha stuck the tracer to the engine.

They had done what they could. It would take investigators months to search every corner of the alien ship. They retraced their steps and crossed the gap between ships. Bertha made sure she was first aboard *Goliath*; she didn't really believe Dean would shut her out to get Rohini alone, but why risk it?

"Okay," he said briskly, after they had shed their suits. "Let's be on our way. You've no idea how boring it was, just sitting here listening to you two jabbering away."

"Don't be in such a hurry, Dean," Rohini said. "There's something I need to check first."

She went to her lab and began adjusting her equipment. Presently a light flashed, and again. She continued to make adjustments, the flashes coming closer together. She was counting under her breath. Despite her outward show of calmness, Bertha realised she was excited underneath. Excited and scared.

Rohini returned to the command area. "It was the radiation around the holes in the derelict's hull that gave me the clue to why my gravity detector didn't work. I've adjusted it accordingly and now it does."

She paused, looking first at Dean, and then at Bertha.

"It's registering some massive gravitational effects in space nearby. We must turn back for Earth and pray we're in time. There's more danger out here than anyone realised—

"Go back?" Dean echoed. "We've hardly started. Our orders—"

"Our orders are not to risk this ship," Bertha reminded him.

"Yes, we must return with what we've learnt—"

"And what's that?" Dean sneered. "You've let a few radioactive holes scare you. Well, I'm not one to run away from danger."

"That ship was riddled with holes, as you saw. And what I believe destroyed it suggested an old hypothesis to account for the dark matter. It's common knowledge that what we see—the stars— represents only about ten per cent of the mass of the universe." Rohini looked thoughtful. "In this case, what you see is not what you get—a universe ninety percent composed of dark matter. Because of this, interstellar space is much more dangerous than anyone thought."

"The hypothesis I referred to suggested that the dark matter is composed mainly of black holes—mini black holes that perforated that ship and went on travelling. And there is no protection against them."

Dean frowned. "We can plug a few holes—"

"If they are a few, perhaps. It looked as if that ship ran into a swarm—and they're not all mini holes. Black holes come in all sizes. My gravity detector registers one nearby with at least a hundred solar masses—not even Bertha's engine will get us out of that kind of gravity well if we're caught in it."

Dean glanced at the screen, doubtful. "I see nothing."

"Of course not. No-one can see a black hole until it's too late."

Bertha began to feel uneasy. She didn't like the idea of cruising through a sea of invisible gravity wells. "We'd better turn around, Dean."

He looked unhappy. Running away was not his style. "Let's not—"

There was a shrill whistle as air rushed suddenly through entry and exit holes. Bertha felt flesh shift on her body as an unexpected gravity tugged at her.

Dean was out of his seat, throwing a sticky patch to her. They each plugged a hole.

Rohini's Geiger clicked rapidly. "Radiation count going up." She looked at Dean. "If we meet a big one..."

Reluctantly he agreed it made sense to turn back, and began to stroking pads to change *Goliath's* course.

Rohini's gravity wave detector was flashing brightly.

"Watch it! I have a gravity signature of more than one thousand gees!"

"I can see it!" Dean exclaimed.

The screen showed a dark circle outlined with a sparkling edge, like a ghost hole in space. "Infalling dust," Rohini commented.

Dean was stroking pads. "Give me max power, Bertha."

She dived for the engine-room. Already her body felt heavy as the ship accelerated. She removed the safety governor to allow power to build up, afraid as she'd never been in her life. If they fell into the hole they would end up as spaghetti.

"What are you doing, Dean?"

"Trying for a slingshot."

She knew what he meant, but her mind wasn't functioning right. It wasn't Dean, it was David. And it wasn't *Goliath* who was skimming close to the hole; speed would build up and they'd be thrown clear. In theory. It was a risky move. Damn macho male, she thought. If they survived, she'd recommend that his sort never be assigned as interstellar pilots.

Then she was flat on her back, muscles tortured and close to black-out.

She shouted, "Get on your acceleration couch, Rohini."

Goliath shuddered and groaned as, seemingly, the ship tried to move in two directions at once. Bertha felt as if her bones had lost their covering of flesh and were grinding one against another. Tidal forces threatened to tear her apart.

The noise sounded as though the ship was breaking up; everything vibrated; fans and pumps whined a protest; lights on the pilot's console flashed red.

Bertha breathed with great effort, as if an elephant squatted on her chest; the blood in her veins was sluggish and reluctant to flow; her sight wavered and she felt dizzy.

The agony of mounting gravity went on till she wondered what she would weigh if, by some miracle, she could crawl onto the scales. There was a smell of...oil? Something had sprung a leak.

The pressure reached a climax and began to fade. Bertha tested her legs; wobbly, but they'd carry her. She struggled upright, found the leak and plugged it. She checked her engine; it had come through without even a minor glitch and she felt proud.

She stepped through into the command area. At the console, Dean looked worn down. He smiled faintly as his fingers moved slowly over the pads, trying to persuade the ship to shed its excess speed.

She soon realised they were already inside the solar system. They'd be getting home a hell of a lot quicker than they'd left.

She went through into the lab. Rohini was still on her couch, looking pale. Blood leaked from her nose. Bertha got the first aid kit, wiped her face and fitted nose plugs.

"Stay lying down, head back. Breathe through your mouth." She dropped a hand onto Rohini's shoulder. "I'll look after you."

Rohini concentrated on breathing through her mouth.

"You're going to be famous. If there are other interstellar ships, they'll have to carry your gravity wave detector as standard issue."

Bertha made coffee and rested, forcing herself to relax. Earth's Orbital Station grew large in the screen and Dean docked. He was grinning, almost his old self, watching Rohini.

As they went through the airlock to the station, he said, "You and me, Ro—we make a great team."

Bertha smiled and linked arms with the younger woman. As they moved away along the corridor, Dean's face darkened in frustration. Rohini glanced back at their pilot and her expression was, perhaps, a trifle wistful.

AFFINITY

by Norman Lazenby

Affinity, n. Relationship, relations, by marriage; relations, kindred, in general; structural resemblance (between animals, plants, languages); (fig.) similarity of character suggesting relationship, family likeness; liking; attraction; (Chem.) tendency of certain elements to unite with others.

His awareness was entirely piscine, coldly alert to the little marine world. His movement was smooth for a while; and then a brisk dart to a sloping rock where he waited placidly, tuned only to living the unthinking existence of an elementary life-form. But it was coolly delightful, utterly non-human, free from mind.

A man passing close to the pond saw the crouching transfixed body of the youth. The man waved his stick.

"Hey, Tom Harper—what yer looking at?"

The young man did not move. He was rigid, unseeing, non-sensing.

"Young idiot! Always starin' at summat," grumbled the old man and he stabbed at the ground with his stick and walked on.

Tom swam around freely as a large dark fish for quite some minutes and then, instinctively sated with the venture, he returned slowly to normality. He straightened and walked thoughtfully away, memories of the shadowy waters retentive to a human mind. He did not brood or indulge in any profound thinking. He was young and he began to whistle and walk jauntily, heading for home and a hearty tea.

As he passed a large field where a number of clucking brown hens strutted around, he did think momentarily of affinity with one of the feathered crowd but he moved on, vigorously attempting to whistle the raucous melody of the latest hit number.

He was crossing a large empty stretch of waste ground when he saw the shapes in the air and he halted, whistle dying, eyes staring, because the grey forms resembled nothing he could recognise. As he waited, his vision raised to the invisible air, his sense of projection towards any living thing smoothed him into nebulous oneness. He was hazily aware of soft cloud against a blue sky and the silence of the empty land; but more and more they were a background to the beckoning, morphological forms.

"Me? You want me?" he whispered. "What are you? I—I don't understand—"

Grey swirls like ten foot high question marks danced gracefully. Tom was sure they were inviting unity, impelling him to use his gift for affinity. But these shapes did not mean anything to him, except that he sensed they contained life.

For the first time in his young career he was afraid of oneness because he could not recognise the being that sought attraction. He hung back, mentally.

Tom Harper knew little of elements, of temporary chemical fusion, of a possible fifth dimension. He knew the living swirls were not dogs or cats, fishes or cows, birds or frogs. He liked the quality of moving animals. A cat was as *great* as a man. A horse was the *equal* of a crow or a schoolboy. A man was no *better* than a duck on a lake, a gull matching wind and sky. Moving creatures were wholly perfect, part of creative force. But these grey beings—what were they? He did not know and he was uneasy.

He walked rapidly over the waste land towards the red roofs of some houses flat against a dip in the ground. As he moved, the swirls urged unison between himself and their entities and they danced like wispy sea-horses in the sky. They were above his head, all around him, silently demanding his presence. He knew they possessed greater intelligence than the other beautiful animals with whom he had had rapport. He knew they wanted to communicate with him, but he was resisting, half-way through the barrier.

A woman appeared through a break in the hedge. She slowly walked across the ground, holding a large basket close to her. Tom watched the woman. When she was near to him, she flicked him a wary glance. He called out jerkily; "See them in the sky, missus!"

She glanced up and annoyance coloured her face. "What are you talking about? Being cheeky?"

He hurried away, even more scared now that he had established that only he could see the question marks bobbing protestingly above him.

He ran home. He entered his room and flung himself on his bed and stared at the ceiling. Scared, he lay in unusual silence for a long time.

The next day he dodged off from the small garage where he worked, took his sandwiches and flask of tea to a nearby wood where he could see the crows wing-flapping high in the trees. Grinning, he watched the clumsy birds and was almost tempted to join them but for the fact that he was hungry.

The grey wispy question marks came like dancing feathers from some distant source. They did not just materialise; they definitely travelled towards him, as if seeking him. Then as they surrounded him like ghostly swirls he knew he would have to give in to their urgency.

Unlike the wonderful animals he often merged with, he had no desire to be one of these unknown shapes, but they *beckoned* so insistently he felt he had to agree.

As his mind swam to the mutual blending point, he heard them speak. Eleven beings spoke at once, without falter and as one, and it wasn't real speech—more of a telepathic junction.

"We seek you…be one of us...only you can help…"

Affinity with these shapes was utterly different to anything else he had experienced. It wasn't like the time he had dissolved into one with a grass snake. And not a bit like being a cat or a dog or any other four-legged creature.

He was a vague, cloudy being—but distinctly *someone.* He was a person. He was a living thing—without a body. He was merging with *someone,* a bodiless entity. He was one shape; not part of the eleven. He could nearly see the others and they weren't so grey and wispy.

"We are Other Self…" transmitted the communal voice. "We are always Other Self…people have an Other Self…don't you know?"

"I – I don't want to see this!" he stammered. "Go away, will you? My job…I should go back…"

"We need you... you must be the only man here who can see us..."

"But I don't really want to!" Fear made him protest; then he began to consider the nebulous individual with whom he had joined. He saw an old shape, male, an image of an old man. Well, this unknown was at least fifty! Yes, the affinity became clearer, focusing into a man, smallish, roundish, grey-haired. This man was clever, with a head full of knowledge. His clothes were indistinct, however.

"You're his Other Self," said the communal thought. "You're not as the man—just his Other Self... you will soon understand... "

Tom Harper nodded, mentally, because he was still sitting near the wood with a flask in his hand. Even as he nodded, he knew the small, roundish, grey-haired man was not nodding—because he, Tom Harper, was not the small roundish man. He was that man's Other Self.

Well, he could see that *now.* He was losing his fear. This wasn't so bad, being another man's invisible, unidentifiable Other Self! No worse than taking the form of a goldfish.

"What do you want me for?" Tom asked. "I mean—you said you need me..."

"Ah—yes. You are Dan Kern's Other Self—at least you are as *one* with his Other Self..."

"Who's Dan Kern? This round little man?"

"Yes. We have selected him for you...as an experiment...because his Other Self is trying to spoil his life..."

"Oh, you are all Other Selfs? Is that it?" He was still perplexed. "Queer—I never seen you lot before—"

"No Real Person can ever see us. We call our Primaries Real Persons... mind you most Primaries are aware of their Other Selfs... but that is all. *You* can see us for the first time because we have moved half-way out of our dimension to meet you. We have assumed these grey shapes—the maximum bodily density we can attain—and even so only you will see them. We exist on a dimension of probability... but enough... You, too, have an Other Self!"

"You mean there's always a person I think I should be? Heck, I think you're right! I sometimes argue with myself and think I ought to be somebody important—like an air pilot—or the captain of a ship—"

"We won't bother with your problems just now, if you please..." came the telepathic voice.

"After all your Other Self is somewhere around. We belong here, with our Primaries."

"You live here?" Tom stared inquiringly at the gyrating shapes. He could see the nebulous beings were really people, men and women, but the details were hazy as one might expect of a reflection, a ghost.

"We are *not* ghosts!" said the voice firmly. "Get that out of your mind..."

"I didn't say that, mister!"

"You thought it... we are genuine Other Selfs... a man or a woman isn't just a body... *everyone* knows that! We live on a dimension an animal body can't attain. We have to... because a man's Other Self is an intangible thing, always wavering, wishing, fighting with him, helping him... saying no or yes..."

Tom Harper looked at the round little man who was the Other Self's Real Person. "Dan Kern? I don't know him. I know a lot of people around Tay Green—Joe Smith, the garage man and Sid Bell, the butcher and plenty others."

"Yes... yes... their Other Selfs are somewhere within call. Please don't confuse us... it's Dan Kern we're concerned about."

Tom glanced again at Dan Kern. It couldn't be real, he thought; it was an image. He was in affinity with Dan Kern's Other Self and naturally the Other Self could always see his Real Person. Yes, he would have to be in touch all the time if he was to be any good as an Other Self.

Dan Kern seemed to be a man with a head full of thoughts. They weren't very nice thoughts

Tom was now Dan Kern's Other Self and Dan Kern's thoughts were quite clear. He was communing with his Other Self, as many men might do when faced with problems.

Dan Kern was asking his Other Self what he should do and the advice handed out by the Other Self was pretty grim. In fact, this intangible being was an unpleasant type.

"Yes, we hate each other," thought Dan Kern. "But kill her—I couldn't do that—could I?"

"You could," communicated his Other Self. "It's easy once you start... you hate your wife... why, you've often thought of killing her... admit that..."

"Well, yes! She's making my life one damned misery. Been like this for years. And now that I've met Ethel the whole thing is unbearable."

"Ah, as you say, your wife knows—knows you've been seeing this woman, Ethel Connor... and divorce is impossible... and not only that, she could ruin you, take her money out of the business. As a solicitor, you'd be exposed to professional humiliation."

"Yes, all that is correct," thought Dan Kern. "I couldn't even go and live with Ethel—she's not that type of woman, thank God!"

"So you'll have to kill Muriel. Think about it. You've got the intelligence. An accident perhaps? Or systematic slow poisoning? She could fall from your boat into the river! Things like this happen every day..."

"Fall from my boat!" thought the small round man. "Ah—that's possible. Muriel isn't very good with boats—"

"You see, you could do it," declared the Other Self. "Get her out of your life. There's money, too... you'd get her money... think about that. Honestly, people are always falling into rivers and getting drowned! If that happened you could think about other things—which would be a change."

Tom Harper stared aghast at the Other Self with whom he was in affinity. The shape danced triumphantly. Tom felt the easy motion; the sense of being almost nothing. The tenuous physical form was just sufficient to prevent dissipation. He realised the Other Self could move, travel, go with its Real Person at will and solid material barriers were of no consequence.

This Other Self was enjoying the mental tussle with its Real Person. Tom could see that Dan Kern was deep in thought. It wasn't actually possible to identify Dan Kern's surroundings but that didn't seem to matter. The man was seated, that much was clear. He was in some room. Beyond that detail faded into a mental mist.

And this Dan Kern wanted to kill his wife! Tom hung in dazed wonder, as disembodied as the Other Self. Now who was Dan Kern? A solicitor! Ah, well, solicitors were people he did not know.

"Now you know the problem," announced the communal voice of the Other Selfs. "Dan Kern's little chat with his Other Self came just at the right time. Dan Kern is not a very pleasant Primary. We've tried to warn his Other Self about the terrible advice he is giving to his Real Person. We can do this because we are all members of this area of life... but Dan Kern's Secondary is really wicked. Always planting, encouraging these murderous thoughts in his Primary's head...and we can't stop it. But you might."

"Me? But—how—how?"

"We've never been able to communicate with ordinary people in the area of life until now. Your talent for affinity is remarkable. We've seen your aurora in our plane before and wondered about it. Let us explain: you're like a visitor to Earth from outer space—such a creature would be an astonishing visitant. And so are you... to us... you are the only Real Person we can talk to... apart from our respective Primaries..."

Nervously, he said: "Well, talk to them about Dan Kern."

"Ah, that is the essence of being a Secondary Self. We can only discuss problems with the Real Person to whom we belong. Actually, we're just mental stooges—some *thing* to answer back and feed strange thoughts. Most of the time we just tell our Primary what he already wants to hear. For instance would-be murderers like to have murderous promptings. We can't talk to Dan Kern. Only his Other Self can do that—naturally!"

"Oh, hell, I don't know that I'll be much good." Tom wished he could escape from this relationship. Already he felt the tug of his own presence. "Do you want me to speak to this Dan Kern—is that it?"

"Of course. Warn him about his Other Self...tell him his Other Self is wicked... tell him you know he wants to kill his wife... that should do some good. He will stop listening to his Other Self—and we will be happy."

They were evidently releasing him from the dimension, for he began a dazed withdrawal, returning to himself as he sat on the grass near the wood. Even as he stared above him, the grey question marks in the sky receded, dwindling at some speed. They were moving on, perhaps to another communal meeting, a place in nowhere.

Unlike his previous merging with the common animals of the countryside, this affair left him somewhat apprehensive. So far he had enjoyed his affinity with other living creatures, understanding their wholeness with their environment. A pig enjoying a messy trough was an expression of perfect creation. A cockerel was a triumphant symbol of fertility. In both, shape and biological function were without fault.

But he was just a young lad, and while he understood animal life like few others could, these grey shapes of a man's secondary self scared him. And now they required him to talk to a man he did not know about a possible murder!

Tom Harper got to his feet, clutched his flask and ran, leaping swiftly over rough ground, vaulting a fence. He approached the garage and shot a last look at the blue sky. The wispy sea-horses had vanished. Thankfully, he dived into the darkish interior of the workshop.

Memories of his thought-conversation with the shadowy images of Man's Other Self lingered in his mind all the afternoon and even impelled him to scan the garage telephone directory. He found the entry: D. Kern & H. Osliff, Solicitors, Tay Green. He noted the street number in the small town.

Tom's young, direct, conscientious mind insisted that he carried out the wishes of the strange projections that existed on the plane of probability. An older person might have wriggled out of the risky commitment. He was a bit afraid, of course, and unsure of himself, but his impressions of the host of Other Selfs were very real. He did not doubt that Man had a personality that could exist on different levels, simultaneously and truly. Oh, he was learning! This was something to think about! What about the queer dimensions some lunatics found when they took LSD?

Late that evening he came to the office and stared at the solid. old door and the plate-glass window with the gilt scroll, Solicitors! He wasn't sure how you talked to a solicitor. Tricky in any case.

For the first time he considered the nature of his possible first remarks to the man.

Hell, it was going to be awkward! He had to tell Dan Kern that his Other Self was wicked—that he had to take no notice of the murderous instincts of his Other Self. He had to warn the man he was thinking of killing his wife! He had to tell the man to stop listening to his terrible second personality.

The enormity of the task suddenly fell around him like a heavy, wet cloak. He was tempted to turn tail. He couldn't do it! He would never find the right words. He wished now he did not have the ability to blend with those intangible doubles on the odd dimension of probability. Those silly Other Selfs had given him a crazy job!

As he hung back, the solid door opened and a small, roundish, grey-haired man took short steps to the pavement. His black hat topped a pudgy pale face. An umbrella was hooked over one arm. His eyes flicked disinterestedly at Tom. At that moment of optical contact the young man impulsively stepped forward.

"Mr. Kern—Dan Kern!" Tom saw in clearer detail the same human figure he had seen when in affinity with the man's Other Self.

"Yes—what do you want?" Cautiously amiable.

"I – I – I've got to talk to you, sir."

"Well—what about? Business to transact?"

"Er—no! Not business. It's hard to explain..."

"Now my young man, I can't be bothered in the street—"

"I—I—I've got to tell you—it's your Other Self! You've got to stop listening to your Other Self!"

The pale skin around the pale eyes crinkled. "What the devil are you talking about?"

"I know your Other Self. I've been sort of in touch with your Other Self, sir, and I know what's going on."

"Going on?"

"Yes. Your second self is pushing you, trying to get you to kill your wife. Now you mustn't listen to it..."

Wariness froze every facial movement. "Why, you young swine—what's the meaning of this? Kill my wife! My wife and I are firm companions!"

"You hate each other. You've been seeing a woman called Ethel Connor. You've thought of arranging an accident on your boat for your wife, Muriel. She won't divorce you. She's got money in this business..."

"Who have you been talking to?" hissed Dan Kern. "This is monstrous—all lies!"

Tom's clear eyes stared into the man. "It isn't all your doing, sir. It's mainly your Other Self shoving these ideas into your head. I—I don't really understand it all—but people have another invisible self. This exists in a dimension that is just probability. I've just learnt all about this, Mr. Kern—and—and I know it sounds strange—but it is part of my being able to achieve affinity with other living things..."

"Affinity!" Dan Kern thrust his set, angry face close to Tom Harper and spat the word. "You damned crazy young hooligan! One more word and I'll send for the police. Kill my wife—indeed! You are mad! If you repeat this to anyone, I'll have you locked up!"

"I had to tell you! I know all about your Other Self. You've got to stop listening to the wicked ideas that your Other Self wants you to do. That's all, Mister Kern. Just let your second self know that you have no intention of harming your wife and it will stop prompting you. Your Other Self is just a stooge, you know. *You* can tell it to shut up..."

Dan Kern grabbed at his umbrella and made to swish it at Tom Harper's legs. The young man was too quick.

Backing off, Tom shouted: "All right—I've told you! I can't do any more! Anyway, I'm sick of it!"

Imprecations bubbled to Kern's lips. "You young pig! I'll get you for this! I'll teach you to slander me!"

Tom Harper made off. Indignant, fed up with the whole business, he made for his home.

Late that night he lay on his bed in his room. Books and tapes littered the floor. A stereo player lay shakily on a pile of magazines. Two pin-ups decorated one wall.

He became aware of the dancing grey shapes assuming an uncertain density just outside his window. He waited expectantly.

The continuations of a man's personality became even more visible and moved like some radiation through the walls and into his room. The small retinue beckoned, urged him to blend. He sensed that Dan Kern's Other Self was of the company. Although he had no real desire to contact these images from the unknown dimension, certain instincts moved him to the state of oneness with the Other Self.

Immediately he tuned into an exchange of thoughts between Dan Kern and his secondary self.

Tom got a faint impression of the solicitor sitting in a room, a blurred place, another Real Person, facing him, a woman, probably his wife "...she just sits...watching me! I wonder what she's thinking. Damn her!"

"You're a fool—putting up with her—" insinuated the Other Self.

"I know—I know! But it isn't easy. That fool of a lad—how did he know? He guessed my mind! Now how could he know! That was uncanny..."

"Forget about him. Just some crazy young fellow! Why don't you get rid of her. Tomorrow! Sunday is a good day to kill people. A boating accident is the best way out..." The secondary self adeptly pointed out all the advantages. "Do it now! Okay? Will you do it?"

Dan Kern glanced at his wife. "Supposed to be reading that blasted book," he thought. But I know she's watching me—hasn't read a damned word for the last ten minutes! God, we hate each other! She's stopping me from seeing Ethel...I could be with Ethel tonight...

"Kill her! She's asked for it!" The sentient image from beyond insisted.

"That damned lad—how did he know?"

"Just chance remarks...no one knows your thoughts but you...and me, *of course...I think you should push her in the river... tomorrow... if no one sees you—well, she just slipped!"*

"Like me—she can't swim!" mused Dan Kern.

"Are you going to do it?"

"Yes. Be damned—I will!"

Evidently the exchange of grim thought ceased. Probably Dan

Kern's attention was brought to bear upon something immediate and real. For Tom it was a blessed relief, but not altogether complete for the communal thought of the dancing Other Selfs crowded at him.

"You see... he has a wicked Other Self..."

"I saw Dan Kern today," protested Tom. "I told him to ignore his bad Other Self. I told him everything. He tried to hit me!"

"We think we have failed, Tom Harper. We shall just allow the Other Self to influence Dan Kern to murder. After all, Dan Kern is his secondary self equally with his primary, and if Real Persons want to kill they usually do. They only argue it out with their Other Self as a means of justifying themselves. Well, it was just an experiment, Tom. You won't see us again. Dan Kern will kill his wife."

The night and early morning elapsed before Tom Harper realised there was possibly one way to save Dan Kern from himself.

If he could only get in touch with Muriel Kern's secondary image, the woman would at least know the grim desires in her husband's mind.

As it was Sunday, he was free to roam the open spaces and quiet streets of the small town. He moved restlessly, seeking some hint of a dancing wispy sea-horse, projecting all his awareness to the sky. After an hour of searching, during which he avoided oneness with a donkey and a wise old dog, he felt faint and out of touch with reality. The Other Selfs were beyond him, it seemed, on their plane of probability, and did not want to come half-way to him. They surely knew he was moving around because they had told him he possessed an aurora.

Apparently they did not want to meet him again.

"Silly things!" he thought. "I only want to help..."

"Why don't you go down to the river?" suggested an inner voice. Of course, the thought was just part of his subconscious and yet it sounded suspiciously like *his* own Other Self!

Was it? He couldn't be sure.

Down at the river, he passed deserted cabin cruisers and a gaudy houseboat before he saw Dan Kern and the woman. A dim memory of the woman as she sat reading last night told him that this was Muriel Kern. This time he saw her in detail; she was stylishly dressed in slacks and jersey. She smoked; leaned against the cabin.

Tom forced her Other Self into a reluctant, slowly-swirling appearance. He swiftly merged with the woman's second entity; a swift transition that brought him oneness with Muriel Kern's Other Self and enabled him to insert thoughts.

"You should talk to your Real Person. Tell her that she's in danger. Her husband intends to kill her... he's going to push her into the river."

"Oh, you're the strange aurora..."

"Never mind about me. I don't know how you'll do it, but get it into Mrs. Kern's head that her husband is definitely set on getting rid of her."

"What good will it do? She knows he hates her..."

"Look," thought Tom, "if she knows he's going to push her into the river, she'll be able to dodge him. See? Then maybe he'll change his mind. Anyway, I'm finished for good with this whole business from now on! I'm off!"

"Nice for you! I'm stuck with Muriel Kern. Well, I *am* Muriel Kern—in a sense—oh, never mind. I'll plant the warning in her mind!"

As he proceeded back home he felt a sense of relief and was once more his light-hearted young self. One thing for sure—he'd never see those fool Other Selfs again! He wanted no part of them. And as the experiment of using one Real Person to warn another Real Person was not exactly a success, quite probably they had no further use for his rare talent.

In future he'd stick to affinity with simple creatures. For instance, a rat could get into some fantastic holes and corners. And the movement of a seagull was a rare thrill.

All the same, it was a bit of a giggle to think he had put a spoke in the wheel of that murderous old fool Dan Kern.

It was simple; Muriel Kern would just keep out of his way and he'd get sick of the crazy idea.

Funny, the way some of these old idiots hated each other! Getting married must be a bit of a mystery!

It was Monday when Tom Harper opened the newspaper, a local evening. He was looking for football news. He didn't intend to read much else.

And then he saw the headline, for Dan Kern was by nature of his profession a prominent man in a small town.

BOATING ACCIDENT

And then he read the rest:

"Late Sunday afternoon a regrettable accident occurred on our local river when Mr. Dan Kern, the well-known solicitor in town, fell from the deck of his cabin cruiser and plunged into the dangerously deep water.

"His body has not yet been recovered..."

HADES WORLD

by Andrew Darlington

Workshop 927 is one of ten moons locked into tight orbit around Hades World. Dropshafts shuttle to its core. Koprowski pauses. Glances over his shoulder shielding his eyes from the corrosive orange glare. The planetary sphere ignites memories, a hidden city, and an exploding 'copter. Two men—Philips and Msimargho murdered, guilt and consequence.

"Dharam wants that world," says Riga. "What she wants she usually gets."

Koprowski smiles in an oddly impenetrable manner. "She won't get it, not this world, not this time."

"She wants answers, solutions, not excuses." Riga shrugs. "She won't like it."

Koprowski turns his back on the planet. Workshop 927 is cool twilight by comparison. The shaft takes him down, away from the surface, away from the dull immensity of space. The co-ordination suites inside the rock purr efficiently. He's conducted still further down. The sound of running water. The faint ghosting of air purifiers. But the expression on the faces of the operators is dour. He feels an aura of apprehension that trembles about them like a physical thing. They fear Dharam's disapproval. And because this tall loose space-bald surveyor brings negative results, arousing her displeasure, they resent him.

He waits outside the final egress, before she accesses him.

The lounge beyond is a labyrinth of artful environment. A garden of coiling greenery, tinkling water cascades. Birds and vivid butterflies spiral in and around gaudy flowers. The overhead walkway takes him round concealed glades and arbours to eventually debouch in an alcove constructed of coloured mica that glows and glistens with its own, and reflected luminance.

Dharam stands with her back to him, absently devoting her

attention to screens that pan across the moon's artificial surface. Crawlers, derricks and hangars sequence through, swimming and winking bewilderingly. Immense gantries as extensive as continents, projectors and coagulators mountain-tall in airlessness.

"Anton Koprowski," she breathes at length. A long slow exhalation of words broken down into their constituent syllables. "You've been here before?"

"No. Not to 927. But I've worked out from several other Shops in other systems, Sirius, Procyon." She knows that. Of course she knows it.

"927 is my worldlet," she says abruptly, turning to face him. Ageless—perhaps in her sixties. Difficult to tell. But she's powerful, and she can be lethal, with an anger that can shake planets. He can tell from every plane and angle of her face. Her family have dominated the Corporation for a century, and despite recent prestige slippage, she retains the habits of absolute authority. "I reserve 927 for personal projects. World Terraformations that particularly interest me. As this one does. You understand that?"

"I understand."

"This world is important to me, Koprowski. I want this planet." Hades world flares across every screen behind her in unison as she speaks. "You know why, Koprowski? You know why?"

"Because this is Earth..?"

They base and dome-up on a shore-side sector of a northern landmass. Radar mapping, thermal probes, and the rest continue through cloud belts that can devour metal. Machines watching diligently from orbital Workshops. But physical survey teams still have some value.

Koprowski's flesh crawls with excited anticipation. He'd half expected landscapes of dead cities, vast desolations of awesome machinery, rusting towers and dereliction. But there's nothing, no sign that this planet was ever inhabited. It's a blighted place blasted clean by hundred-k-a-second weather systems, temperatures peaking at 380C, with a high ever-present smog of sulphuric acid droplets that descend during chill moonless nights leaving a heavily toxic dew. Looking inland there are startles of continuous lightning, electromagnetic impulses that illuminate the boiling underbelly of cloud in ferocious strobe-patterns. Beyond which the horizon runs with heat-dance like brilliant liquid.

Suited and insulated from it all Koprowski watches. It's bad. A devil's breath of radiation, murderously high with infra-R's and ultra-V's. But he's done worse. There's no real problem, just a matter of selecting appropriate technical procedures. Given ten years of concentrated planetary bio-engineering, oxygenation, and systems rehabilitation Earth could be a fine place to raise your kids.

They jet-copter the continent from the vast heat-shimmering dust bowl at the centre, to the ring of raw mountains at the tectonic rim, then back to the dome. Atmospheric readouts say 95% carbon dioxide. The rest is a stew of nitrogen, oxygen, sulphur dioxide and slight water vapour. A system that's remained stable for 7,000 years. The oceans are an unexpected bonus. At some stage in the environmental meltdown, as the surface water evaporated to be expelled into space, a crust of salt, grainy wind-blown oxidised grit and—to a certain extent, decayed organic matter, had sealed over and preserved what remained.

With dusk gathering the ten-man team are filing reports to 927, to the rest of the moonlet grid, and beyond to Central Galactic Data Core. Duties complete, with time to kill, and an itch to physically experience the strangeness, Koprowski accompanies Schroter to the beach. The glare dulling, the clouds hurtling so high and so deadly. They have a monstrously non-human beauty. A sky that's still a fire-storm curdled with cerise and artery slits of crimson roiling into a vortex of iridescence. This alienness is the frisson he craves like a drug, despite the fact that by his being here, he's ensuring its end. Its transformation into bland human uniformity.

Yet this is Earth. Somewhere higher than the clouds, higher than the artificial terraforming moons, there is Luna. The legendary satellite that was the first human destination in space, now forever invisible. Darkness here will be dark, with only lightning to populate its blackness.

The ocean crust, seen so close, heaves unpleasantly. A rippling amoeba that undulates on, apparently forever.

"Hey Anton, watch me walk on water." Schroter ventures out onto it, dancing clumsily, a stocky and irreverent man, heavily suited, but the crust is dense and deep.

Spokes of mauve begin irrigating a more sullen ochre sky. Koprowski eases his visor filter back by degrees. Behind him the dome is ebon. The 'copter apron, and a spider-work of projectors that can rip continents apart or raze mountains.

He grins. Schroter is loping in a graceless parody of some Tri-vid dance routine.

A sudden burst of lightning storms in shock waves. It drenches the world in luminous after-images. And when everything restabilises, Schroter is no longer there...

"It seems incredible to us, moving in a community of a thousand worlds, that they had but a single planet." Dharam speaks to the images on the screens. "We have separate worlds for agro-business, chem-extraction, and every other process essential to the maintenance of civilisation. They were forced to do it all within the confines of the one eco-system. No wonder they reduced it all to poisonous ash. But by then it no longer mattered. By the time Earth's mineral and energy resources were exhausted and the biosphere was shot, the deplaneting phase was well under way."

Koprowski waits, shuffling nervously. Repeating 'I know all this' beneath his breath. What about Phillips and Msimargho? When's she going to mention *them*? He can still see the cross-hairs on the enhanced target image of their receding 'copter. He can still feel his thumb on the firing stud.

"It's been 7,000 years, Koprowski, since final contact. And I often wonder who were the last humans to quit the mother world. And where did they go? Did they resettle on the small forest world we passed on the way in, the one called Mars? Or perhaps they came further and just got absorbed into the galactic mainstream? No one knows. Or cares. But Earth still carries that emotive charge. An after-taste unlike that of any other. Our rivals—'Planetary Transformations', aim to steal our status. I hear reports that they're sinking piles into an as-yet unspecified neutron star to construct a hub city there, a luminous showcase of just how technically proficient they are. A stunt like that could destroy our credibility and seriously erode our own share of the market. So we go one better, we get the jump on *them*. We rehabilitate Earth and make this our hub of operations. In real terms, a very minor operation, but in publicity value it'll wipe them out of existence."

"But we can't do it. It's not possible."

"*Can't*? We do whatever pleases us. We construct continents suspended in gas giants. We take ice worlds, and we ignite their moons into artificial suns. We take superheated planets and we build new thermospheres to tame them. There's nothing we can't do. *Nothing*."

Koprowski breathes deep in the cloister coolness and begins. His memories bone-bright ...

Earth night fills with spectres. Flood-beams and flash-rods battle an almost physical darkness of heaving ocean-crust writhing with liquid shadow. Armoured Crawlers gyrate across its unstable surface, sensors probing every direction, hunting weak points, fissures, blow-holes, but finding none. Suited men are strung out in their wake. The shifting weirdness illuminated intermittently by a perpetual lightning icing it all to brief electric clarity.

It's been hours since Schroter's disappearance. Each moment thickens the night into more awful threat. Hard to believe that above all this there's clean clear space, and ten working moonlets that have shuttled from the stars, watching it all like impotent gods. As night thickens here there's only primal starless dark.

The lead Crawler is the next to go. Jaws open in the crust beneath it. Geysers of superheated steam jet hundreds of metres into the air. The cat-tracks scream as the vehicle cants vertiginously. Koprowski is slouching some way back, his suit pencil-beams pick out every detail. Fear hits him like a knife thrust, he's screaming into his visor, watching the car settle slowly and inexorably through a sudden pit that's belching poisonous effluvium. Until the crust heals over, leaving no trace of Crawler, or crew.

"Back," howls Koprowski over the interlink. "Get the hell back Dome-side, and do it *fast* !"

Cars whine into reverse, their floods scything across rippling waves of grit debris. His guts have liquefied, he's uncomfortably sweat-damp despite his suit thermostats. Sudden fissures rip across the rolling terrain, flash-rods punch glaring holes through hard blackness. Running lurching men are silhouettes. Then the crust beneath Koprowski's feet dissolves to nothing. He's face-down and sprawling in a thick noxious mire, thrashing at its receding rim. But sinking slowly, something pulling him into its dreadful maw, lapping up around his face-plate claustrophobically. Until he submerges. Sinking like a stone towards the dead heart of the wasted land.

"They take me down in a kind of weird dreamlike silence for almost an hour. The sludge beneath the surface gradually thins until we emerge into the clean ocean that exists below. What they used to call the mid-Atlantic trench. There's natural light down there, forests of plants and a million fish species. The city we reach at length is flecked with phosphorescent towers and translucent bridges spanning spiral spires of fantastically graceful architecture, and ..."

"What are they *like*?"

"They're something like dolphins. Something like people. But ultimately like neither. They're indescribably beautiful, and I get the impression they could knock our moonlets out of the sky with a single thought."

"A new species can't evolve in just 7,000 years."

"No. But existing species can mutate and adapt to rapidly changing conditions, particularly when those changes involve exposure to heavy doses of unshielded radiation."

She turns slowly, deliberately. "And they let you go?"

"They want nothing from us, other than to be left alone."

They explode up onto the beach close to their vanishing point. The Crawler, Schroter, Koprowski, intact and unhurt. Through senses momentarily confused by the abrupt glare of ghastly light they watch the jet-copter hurl from the dome apron and out over the ocean. A comet of incandescence. With some awful sense of foreboding the two heavily suited men lurch clumsily for the base through burnt-out salmon sand. Blood leaps hot and the beating of Koprowski's heart is a painful thing.

"Anton? What...!" as they burst into the Comm Suite. "We thought they'd killed you."

"No time for explanations now. Who's in that 'copter, and what're they doing?" yells Koprowski.

"Phillips and Msimargho, they're dropping a Daddy Mack onto the mid-Atlantic trench. That baby'll rip the crust so wide it'll vape the sea into one huge typhoon of steam. By the time the crust heals over whatever nasties are lurking down there will be *extinct*."

Koprowski digests the information. "Has data on these life-forms gone to 927?"

"Routine stuff has been logged as normal, but it'll still be percolating up there."

"Then get it out now to Central Galactic Core—on priority band, while I recall that 'copter. *Do it*!"

The Comm operator, galvanised and a little afraid of Koprowski's urgency, moves as instructed while the link to the 'copter opens. There are squalls of static.

"Either it's not getting through to them," from Schroter, "or they're deliberately ignoring us and going in for the kill."

"Stay with it." Koprowski hurls himself from the suite and down the corridor to a separate console. Tunes in the cross-hairs on the enhanced image of the receding 'copter, focusing a power that can raze mountains. His thumb on the firing stud. His throat pebble-dry at what he's contemplating, raw with tension. His breath catches in his throat, where it stays. There are two men in the speeding craft, their lives balanced against the survival of a sentient species.

"No response!" yells Schroter down the corridor. "They've picked up my command, but they're ignoring it. They're gonna complete the mission regardless."

Koprowski's thumb goes in. The lethal charge leaps in the 'copter's wake. The detonation sun-bright against darkness ...

"We can't touch Earth. It's no longer our world. It belongs to them now." The words come with just a hint of triumph, despite the dryness at the back of his throat. Dharam wants this world, and like Phillips and Msimargho, she'll certainly not hesitate at genocide to achieve her aim, if that option were still open. But he's taken care to ensure the authorities beyond the system are alerted to the new circumstances, he's logged it all with Central Galactic Core. She'll not dare act against them. He's made sure of it.

"You destroyed Corporation property—namely the jet-copter, and murdered two of my employees to ensure the survival of your precious new subaquatic species?"

For the first time Koprowski looks away. "That's what disturbs me. I was prepared to do it, yes. I programmed and launched the charge. I admit that. But it wasn't me that exploded them. That 'copter blew itself out of the sky before my charge hit them. A good second before it hit them. You don't have to take my word for that, Vid records will confirm it."

"You mean your friends beneath the crust are responsible?"

He nods numbly. "They're quite capable of self-defence."

For a very long moment Dharam is silent, ignoring his presence, as though the interview is over. He turns.

"Anton Koprowski," she breathes at length. "Can I ask you one more question?"

He waits.

"Do you realise the full import of what's been done here?"

"I think so, yes."

"So what happens when your amphibious friends down there decide *they* need living space out among the stars? Have you thought of that Koprowski, have you? Can you imagine our thousand planets re-made like *that*?"

The multiple image of Hell-World Earth swims on the screens behind her. He watches with skin-crawling fascination ...

“SOMETHING”

by Eric C. Williams

Six months after I buried my wife I moved to an old cottage some two hundred miles from the scene of her accident. It was the furthest point I could find away from the blow that had wrecked me. The cottage had been a Welsh farmer’s home, high on poor ground at the head of a valley. The farmer had aged beyond caring for the sheep that cropped the boggy tops and his sons had gone chasing civilisation in the coastal towns. I got it all cheaply, together with the weekly services of a postman who brought up newspapers from the valley (since I wrote no letters or received any), and a motorised grocer who kept us fed and supplied with odds and ends. Here I brooded, and my daughter, Poppy, chased chickens.

We had named our child Poppy because it was an old-fashioned name and we liked old-fashioned things. She was eight when her mother died and I had to uproot her and transplant her in the strange ground of a minute Primary school in mid-Wales. I took her each morning down to the road running across the bottom of the valley and there we waited until the school bus came along collecting all the outlying children. We talked as we waited, and one bright, cool morning as we sat on the stone wall by the road she asked me, “Daddy, what are the holes for in my bedroom wall?”

“What holes, dear?”

“They weren’t there yesterday, Daddy. Did you do them last night?”

I looked at her. Her grey eyes blinked peacefully at me with the trust of nine years. I concentrated on what she had said to me.

“No,” I answered. “What do you mean? What sort of holes?”

“Big holes.” She held up her hands, cupped together to show how big the holes were.

"Are you sure?" I asked stupidly. "How many?"

"Three," she answered cheerfully. "By my bed. What are they for?"

I shook my head. It was difficult for me to be sure whether the conversation was meant to be a game or was serious. There had been an evening two months before when Poppy had come running in from the outhouse where she kept a rabbit to drag me out to see a "something." A *something!* She wouldn't or couldn't say what a "something" was, and when we entered the outhouse she was tickled to find the "something" had become a "nothing."

I didn't appreciate her childish joke. Were the "holes" another joke? I didn't want to be as grouchy as I had been about the "something" so I told her I would repair the holes during the day.

"It must be mice," I told her and she gave a shriek of delight.

"I hope so," she said. "I love mice... but they must be very big mice."

How big I was startled to find when I got back to the stone house and climbed the narrow staircase to her bedroom. Over the head of the simple pinewood bed were three identical recesses almost like the box shaped holes found in some old cottage room walls where candles or lamps might be placed.

These holes, however, were not plastered and painted—they were raw granite about six inches square and deep and glistening with a glass-like finish. No mouse cut those holes, nor a mason of these arts; the craftsmanship was amazing: the deep corners of the holes were as clean and sharp as those of a tin box. I gave up that mystery and tackled the easier one of why I had never seen the holes before.

Admitted I did not come to Poppy's room every day (I left her to make her own bed and to sweep up), but there was no possibility that the holes had been made during our tenancy, therefore they must have been there all along but covered over.

I looked behind the bed for evidence of fallen plaster or, perhaps, painted paper that might have peeled from the cavities. There was nothing but fluff. I scratched my head then banished the problem as something vaguely to do with cottage industry of the remote past...sockets for some primitive weaving machine. I sat one of Poppy's dolls in each of the holes and went about my lonely chores.

I mention these seemingly unimportant things because I believe they were the first manifestations of...something.

Twice more over the next year, Poppy tried the "something" joke on me.

"It's back," she cried from the doorway. "Come and see."

With not so simulated wrath I went across the muddy yard to the outhouse. The "something" had gone.

"Oh!" said Poppy. "What a shame!"

"What is this game?" I asked after the third run. "What is this nothing-something supposed to look like?"

Her grey eyes looked past me considering. "I don't know, Daddy, really. It's kind of wobbly like water."

"Wobbly like water!" I said sarcastically. "You're sure it wasn't solid like steam?"

She looked at me wonderingly. I wasn't surprised she didn't understand my ill-tempered sarcasm.

"No," she said. "It was like water, only not wet."

"What? A bucket of it?"

"No. There, in the air. Just there." She took a pace and showed me where the something had been. "It was a square of it."

I flapped my hand at her and walked out.

A good long time after that, when Poppy was on her last year at a school where she stayed all week and only came home at weekends, we had another occurrence. I kept a few chickens in the yard, almost you might say, on the hillside because they easily hopped over the dry-stone wall in summer and went grubbing in the grass beyond, and one gets accustomed to their occasional uproars and peculiar calls from all kinds of corners and directions. But one morning a whole chorus of shrieks and flapping of wings sent me running from the kitchen to the yard.

I expected to see a fox or even a wild cat chasing the chickens, but what I saw were the chickens chasing a chicken. For a second that is what I saw, then I saw what the chickens saw: the quarry had the body of a chicken and the head of a nightmare.

The head was so fantastically distorted that I thought the chicken had got its head jammed inside the viscera of some rotten carcass, and was running, blindly around the yard. But it wasn't running blindly; it could see all right. It fluttered to the top of a pile of stones, then to the top of the open outhouse door and balanced there fighting off its frantic fellows who flung them selves into the air with ridiculous lack of control.

I gazed at the thing, gulped down my bile, then reached back into the kitchen for my shotgun and blew the head from the cursed thing. The chickens tore the rest of it to pieces.

I was so upset by this disgusting piece of horror that when the postman called the next day I mentioned it to him. He was a merry, obliging little Welshman and generally did his best to lift me out of the introspective gloom in which I passed my days.

"You don't say, now!" he exclaimed and he didn't grin as I expected him. He studied the ground at his feet. "You're sure it's not one of these mutations? I've read they can be awful, you know."

"Of course it wasn't," I told him. "Mutations don't appear overnight. And don't ask if it was somebody else's chicken wandered in; I had twelve and now I've got eleven."

"Um," he said and turned his eyes towards the distant hills. "Evans shot his cat ten or more years ago. That was a nasty business, too."

"Which Evans?" I asked brusquely. "And how do you mean 'nasty?'"

"Old Evans you bought the farm from: Evan Evans: lived here with his boys. You know."

"Him?" I grunted. "And what happened? What's it got to do with my chicken?"

The postman took off his cap and let the wind ruffle his hair.

"Evans loved the cat. It was his wife's, really, but she slipped on that scree slope up there and smashed her head in one winter out looking for sheep, so Evans looked after the cat after that. Very sad it was."

"The cat was sad?" I asked caustically.

For a moment it looked as if he might grin but then he shivered and pursed his mouth in distaste. "No; her. A good-looking woman she was but the stone smashed her head flat, so it was said, flat as a pancake. Old Evans carried her home and the boys laid her out in the bedroom. The Coroner's wife told my wife he'd never seen anything like it outside of a pressed-meat shop window."

"But what about the cat?" I asked impatiently.

For a moment it looked as if my postman was regretting his impulse to tell me about Evans's cat. He put on his cap, adjusted the bag strap on his shoulder and gave his bicycle a jerk.

"I never saw it, mind you, but man, I smelled it!" He did chuckle then, but ghoulishly.

"Smelled it a mile off as I was coming up here that day. Old Evans was burning the head of his cat. Burning it, not burying it. I asked him politely like whether he'd never heard of pollution. I tell you it was a regular stink! But he was in a proper sweat, man, like you in a way, and he told me.

"Cut its head off he had, buried the body out on the hill and burnt the head where it had fallen here in this yard. 'Why?' I asked him. 'Why d'you do such a terrible thing to a poor cat?' And do you know what he did, boyo? He was *sick!*

"Evan Evans, as tough an old bird as they come—he was sick just thinking about it. 'Ah!' he says, and he spit on the fire. I was never able to get him to tell me what was wrong with the cat's head. Like your chicken I expect."

After the postman had gone I began to feel very jumpy, prowling round the place, opening shed doors and peeking inside, listening outside rooms before going in, looking over my shoulder.

I couldn't settle. Evening came on and I began doing the rounds again. I went upstairs to Poppy's weekend bedroom and stared at the three holes in the wall. She didn't have dolls in them now—some sort of aromatic candles. I went to the outhouse and pushed back the creaky door. In the dim interior something quivered over by the rabbit's cage as if air was rising from an intense fire. But the disturbance wasn't generally distributed, it was confined to one block in mid-air about six inches by six inches. I squinted and then jerked back as the rabbit gave a terrible squeal and thrashed against the wire front of its box. In the dim light I could see its head inside the block of heat waves and it was turning inside out. Slowly the bloody interior and the brains were squeezing out of the head's orifices.

My heart suddenly accelerated and cold sweat poured down my face; I was terrified, no, perhaps *horrified* is the best word. The rabbit still lived. I couldn't look: it was too ghastly.

I ran back to the house with my hands over my ears, bolted the door, and was sick in the kitchen sink. When my heart had slowed a little I was able to think.

This was the 'something' that Poppy had seen. My God! She was due to come home tomorrow. I could not possibly send a telegram in time to stop her. I would have to meet her down at the road and tell her to go back to school.

No, that was impossible: what could I say to her? The farmhouse was burnt down; anthrax reported; the 'something' was back and turning the livestock inside out. I twisted and trembled all night and only when the sun was well up did I unbolt the door and creep across the yard with the gun to the outhouse. There was nothing in the bright air, but a ghastly thing still stirred in its cage. I blasted it from six feet sway then built a fire outside and burned the thing cage and all.

Poppy came back a woman in all except age and saw instantly that I was ill. She took over the house and would not listen to my arguments that she should get away to London and start to carve out a civilised life for her self.

"I am not leaving, Daddy," she said gently. "I am going upstairs to unpack then you are going to have a good sleep on that couch while I bake some bread. You haven't been looking after yourself."

She came down in ten minutes and blew a kiss in my direction.

"I see you've made another hole in the wall above my bed," she said. "Very useful. Just right for my cosmetics."

I gaped at her, then jammed shut my trembling jaws.

The next day I was in a state close to panic and followed her everywhere until ordered firmly to rest. The day following I kept up a less obvious surveillance—although she gave me many pensive smiles as if wondering if I was not only underfed, but out of my mind.

Every succeeding day was better. I explained away the death of her rabbit and the dreadful image faded from the front of my mind. Occasionally I had bad dreams and woke up gasping, but life slipped at last into its old deep rut along which we both jogged.

Two years passed, and then a Christmas. We had spent a snow-isolated day in sweet accord, clearing snow, eating well, listening to the radio, reading the books we had given each other, and finally drinking our own preferred beverages and smoking.

We kissed each other goodnight at midnight. The cottage had three bedrooms upstairs, one large one, which had been Evans and his wife's room, and two small rooms into which his sons had been squeezed. The large room was now mine and one of the smaller Poppy's. The other I had converted into a bathroom. I climbed into my creaky bed drowsy with food, smoke and drink. I had no premonitions. I think I slept almost instantly.

I was woken by a shriek so loud and terror-filled I think my heart stopped for a second. I couldn't think although I knew Poppy was shrieking 'Daddy, Daddy!' My body was as stiff as if I had slept in the snow outside—I know my fingers were numb—for several seconds I could not move. And then my limbs reacted of their own accord and I lurched out of bed in a mess of sheets and crashed into the chair I kept near for my clothes. The pain woke me from my half trance.

"All right, Poppy!" I shouted. I got to the door then cursed and went back to the chair for the torch I always had hanging there. I ran to the door, across the narrow landing, and tore open the door to Poppy's room. She was standing by her bed with her hands up to her head. *But it wasn't a head...*

Oh, my God! How can I describe it? The chicken had been ghastly, the rabbit awful; this was worse. The shimmering cube was not large enough to encompass all her head; it had seized on the centre of her face. All that had changed, and round it hung Poppy's gorgeous hair while her creamy neck supported such a monstrosity that I fell backwards out of the room adding my own shrieks to hers.

The torch fell to the floor and continued to send a beam along the oak boards towards the stairs. Along this pathway of escape I squirmed like a frantic lizard and went headfirst down the ancient stairs. I felt no pain from the collisions my knees and elbows made with the steps and in the darkness downstairs I smashed into a door jamb and didn't feel that either. But it told me where I was and with a swipe of my arm I found the spade we always kept by the front door in winter in case snow had to be cleared away.

I turned about towards the glow of my torch above and like a puppet controlled by a palsied puppeteer I climbed the stairs and approached the back opening of Poppy's room. Sounds still came out of it but they were low, gobbling sounds that made me want to retch just to imagine what orifice could make them.

I picked up the torch and shone it through the door. She was on the floor crawling towards me. The cube had finished with her head and was working on the shoulders. Before my eyes she began to liquefy.

There is a. blank. The insane rage that takes over sometimes when we have to squash a large spider swept me and drowned me. I killed her and went on killing her until suddenly I had no more strength. I flung away the spade and stood looking at my work, still holding the torch.

Amongst the awful mess the watery cube still glistened and rippled as if feeding. I had not the strength to wield the spade—not that blows hurt it—but my revulsion was so great that mindlessly I flung the torch at it. Instantly there was a blinding flash and an enormous explosion that ended my consciousness for some minutes. Heat and smoke revived me—in fact, my clothes were alight from the conflagration in the room. I dragged myself to the door and stood looking into the flame lit room.

Nothing remained of Poppy. Nothing. Nor of the cube. The flames raced around the room and began eating the landing floor where I stood. The cottage was built of granite and timber and with a magnificent roar the fire began to eat it all.

The village firemen found me the next morning sitting with my back to the yard wall staring at the heap of smoking rubble that was Poppy's grave.

"Propane explosion," they said to each other.

"Something," I muttered. *"Something... Nothing."*

ADVENT

by Sydney J. Bounds

Baron sat on a crumbling weed-covered doorstep, a big knife in his wrinkled hand. For years he had used the knife to whittle wood; there had been a demand for his ear-plugs, carved to fit each individual ear so that no sound leaked through. That demand had just about ended, but he felt safer with a knife in his hand.

He stared along the suburban street to what had been a main road, listening. Most of the houses were empty, the air still and quiet. No sales jingles; they had just about finished too. No swish of bicycle tyres as bored youngsters went looking for fun; their idea of fun too often developed a fatal aspect. The law, like his doorstep, had crumbled away.

He wondered if he should go shopping, but the Eaties had only the same tasteless mush and it became harder to force it down; but there was nothing else unless he cultivated a taste for weeds. At least it was free.

Odd that he should suddenly think of money after all these years. Credit, that was the word. At the Eaties, everything was on credit. Not that there was much to buy these days; the world seemed to have run down and nobody cared any more. It was easy to forget the way things had been now he was past seventy.

He really ought to go to the Eaties; there was still a chance of something different. And there might be another of the old gang to talk to, anyone to stop his vocal chords from rusting completely. He eased off the doorstep, joints stiff, and moved into the centre of the street and walked slowly towards the main road. He ought to stock up. Getting about wasn't getting any easier; he sighed for the days when a bus still ran occasionally.

Of course, the kids took the situation for granted. They'd grown up with it and had never known anything else. A memory came to mind, the way it had started.

The experts got it wrong. The signal from space didn't come on the twenty-one centimetre band; it howled across every radio wavelength. World-wide, radio telescopes were blasted by such powerful pulses that amateurs built small dish antennae in their gardens to pick up the broadcast. Now it was a question of "Who's there?"

The transmission drove astronomers wild because it interfered with research programmes. The media had a field day with every sci-fi cliche they could dig out of TV videos, games and comics; one tabloid went so far as to reproduce the gaudy covers of long-forgotten pulp magazines. Even Wells got a mention.

Martians are Real!

The Little Green Men are Coming!

Saucer People talk to Us!

Baron had just quit his job as copywriter to set up his own agency, Howard Baron Associates, with one writer and an artist. He was young and pushy with big ideas, and first contact seemed like an omen. How could he turn it to his advantage? What products could benefit from an extraterrestrial angle?

It was a great time, a time of excitement and wonder. After the signal came the message.

* * * * * * * *

He was puffed by the time he reached the Eaties and saw rusting bicycles stacked outside. He shuffled into the cafe just inside the entrance where a group of youngsters sat around a table.

"You smell anything?" one asked, holding his nose.

Baron's fingers felt for the handle of the knife clipped to his belt.

An older person sat apart, gripping a stick. "This coffee gets worse," he complained.

"Coffee's coffee, Mac," Baron said, and punched a button on the machine. A dark liquid poured onto the floor.

A titter of laughter came from a young girl. "You're supposed to hold a cup under it, grandpa!"

Baron put a tin mug under the spout and pressed the button again. He took his coffee to Mac's table and sat down.

"Not to worry," Mac said. "I forget things all the time."

Baron sipped his coffee—it was barely warm without milk or sugar—and watched a puddle spread beneath the machine.

"Why doesn't the cleaning thing take care of that?"

Mac shrugged. "Haven't seen one the last few times I've been in. Seems everything's breaking down"

They sat in a companionable silence for a while, then Mac said, "Remember teevee?"

* * * * * * * *

Baron had a television set in the office to study his rivals' ads. The screen showed a panel of assorted experts debating the signal from space.

"Obviously it does not come from Mars."

"No, it's travelled nearly fifty light-years, from a planet orbiting another star in this galaxy."

"An extraordinarily powerful broadcast—"

"And that suggests the senders have some source of energy far beyond anything we have."

"So even if we could let them know we've received their transmission, they wouldn't get our reply for another fifty years."

Baron scribbled on a pad: why wait fifty years? Contact us now!

On-screen, a gofer pushed a sheet of paper into the chair-person's hand. She glanced at it, looked out at him and exclaimed:

"*News Flash!* The signal has stopped. What is assumed to be a message is now running in its place. First indications are that it is in binary code and mathematicians are already working to break the code. Now we really are listening to the stars!"

* * * * * * * *

After coffee they entered the main store. The aisles were almost as empty as the shelves and the high roof made it a place of echoes. Dust gathered on empty racks.

Baron cleared his throat. "Place is as big as an aircraft hangar."

Mac snorted. "When was the last time you saw an airplane?"

Baron began to feel depressed as he looked at a row of packets the shape and size of family-size soap powders; they tasted like that too.

The loud-speakers were silent, and no-one bothered to change the peeling posters now:

Three for the price of two!

The cheapest and the best!

You'll never try another brand after trying ours!

Baron pulled a tatty plastic bag from his pocket and filled it from what little choice there was. Sometimes he felt sure that exactly the same stuff was in each packet, despite the different brand names. Suspiciously, every packet carried the same instructions: just empty into a bowl and add water.

They made their way to the exit, where Mac paused. Baron's eyes followed his gaze. Grinning youths, riding their bicycles in circles, waited for them.

Baron touched the handle of his knife. "Looks like we've got trouble."

* * * * * * * * *

Baron studied a Xerox of the decoded message and wondered if he should. The message was a set of instructions. Various people in positions of authority had tried to stop the message spreading, but it was too simple, too easy. Anyone could follow the instructions to build an alien device. Engineers did, in laboratories; backyard inventors did too.

Pretty soon the things were everywhere; bobbing up and down on city pavements, dancing along country lanes. And not just here; all around the world they danced and sang their jingles. "Jingle Djinns" the tabloids named them. No human control was possible.

Most people were amused, but Baron wasn't. They were stealing the bread out of his mouth, because the alien message was a sales pitch, advertising in the local language of each country.

The jingles said, "Buy now, pay later."

They said, "You want it now. Why wait?"

"You must have our latest."

"You'll like our version better."
"We have only satisfied customers."
"Another wonder product from your friendly ET."
"Buy one, get one free."
They said, "Remember, we give unlimited credit."
Howard Baron snarled, "Market conmen – that's all they are!"

* * * * * * * *

"Five against two," Baron said. "We'll be all right if we stay together." He walked slowly beside Mac along the main road; fortunately, they lived in the same direction.

The youngsters followed, pedalling furiously, buzzing them. It was a game to see who could count coup by touching the back of a head as they wheeled past.

Baron put up with it as long as he could. To draw his knife would excite them; things could get out of hand and develop dangerously, and the kids had quicker reflexes.

"Little devils," Mac panted, flailing his stick at them.

They were all of school age, three boys and two girls, but there were no longer any schools. They had nothing to do except amuse themselves.

Baron reached an overgrown garden where weeds swept down to the road. Tall spiky weeds amid a tangle of ivy and bramble, broken glass and splintered wood from what had once been a greenhouse. He discarded his plastic bag.

"Come on," he said, and drew his knife. He swung it like a scythe, slashing a way through. "They'll have a lob to follow us in here."

He pressed on as fast as he could, realising that he was badly out of condition. Mac followed at his heels, grumbling. Angry voices sounded behind them because the cycles, old tyres filled with grass, juddered over ruts in the ground and spilled their riders. Pursuit fell away.

"They'll be waiting for us when we come out," Mac said.

* * * * * * * *

Public amusement became uneasiness when it became clear that the Jingle Djinns could replicate themselves. Scientists were first disbelieving, then startled, then baffled; the original models had seemed so simple.

Too late it was realised that simplicity hid complexity. Too late a law was passed forbidding anyone to build more of them.

The Earth was swamped by dancing alien machines, deafened by a cacophony of jingles. "Buy, buy, buy," they chanted, night and day, louder and louder as their numbers multiplied. "Coming to this town real soon now!" It drove people mad; it was no longer funny because there seemed no way to stop them.

Baron lost his temper and drove his car at one, but it dodged him easily. A few were destroyed by angry mobs who surrounded them, but they could breed faster than they were destroyed. The government consulted the military and an exercise was planned.

* * * * * * * *

Baron parted tall weeds, peered out and sighed. "You're right, Mac."

He saw the gang's cycles piled up in a heap. They had broken off branches of trees to make clubs and were busy smashing old fencing, window frames and anything else they found breakable.

"I've got my stick, Howard."

"We need some kind of distraction—luckily they've got a short attention span."

At one time, Baron had prided himself on his quick thinking; it paid to be one step ahead in the ad game. And he could still think better than most, even if it took longer the older he got.

"Follow me, and keep close," he said, and stepped into the open.

He and Mac got halfway there before a young one spotted them. "Wrinklies!"

There was a disorganised rush. Baron swung his knife and the first boy dived sideways at the ground, swearing.

"Run," Baron shouted. "It's not far!"

Mac lumbered behind, lashing out with his stick. "What's not far?"

Baron reached his objective, an open ditch. The ground was still soggy at the bottom, he observed. He stood over the ditch, knife poised; then plunged it down as hard as he could. It stuck, and he wrenched it sideways, to and fro.

It pulled loose—and a geyser of water sprayed upwards, drenching them all.

"Beat it quick, Mac," Baron urged.

The kids watched the geyser as if hypnotised. They jumped in and out of the water, laughing like hyenas.

"They've never seen anything like that," Baron said, sorry to have lost his secret cache. He'd found one of the old water-pipes days ago, one that still held some of the precious liquid. A dreadful waste, but it gave him time to get away unscathed.

* * * * * * * *

What saved the Jingle Djinns were the new machines they built. Physicists went paranoid trying to figure out how these worked.

Baron tried the nearest one. He had reams of confidential paperwork and it cost to have it shredded. But the new machines apparently worked with anything. He dumped it in the open maw and pushed a button and a can of drink popped out; it looked and tasted like cola.

The next generation of machines had a dial, for drinks, food bars, or toys. The kids loved them. As public anger died away, the proposed military exercise was abandoned.

People approved of the new machines. They liked using them to get rid of unwanted junk and get back something new. Scientists talked about rubbish being reduced to its component atoms and then being reconstituted in another form.

Eventually the machines produced more and more items: household goods, furnishings, clothing, all free. Eggheads wondered where it would all end…

* * * * * * * *

Baron escorted Mac home. Mac was not happy. "All that water," he mumbled. "You were keeping it for yourself."

"Lock the door and keep quiet. You don't want them to know you're here."

"Things can only get worse," Mac said gloomily.

Baron returned to his house by a roundabout route, looking back all the time to make sure he wasn't followed. It was a blow losing the water, but he still had rainwater in his roof tank.

The extra exertion had made his muscles ache. He wanted to sit down with a nice cup of tea...tea? His mind was wandering again. There hadn't been any tea for years.

He reached his front door and pushed. It swung open easily. Too late he realised the gang was waiting inside for him.

* * * * * * * *

For once, the eggheads were right. When people could get anything they wanted free, by pushing a button, factories shut down, shops closed and unemployment rose.

One of the first things to go, ending Baron's career, was television; there was nothing to advertise after the economy crashed and money lost its value. His clients disappeared overnight.

Alien machines took over the commercial channels, satellite and cable, promising "Anything you want, we will provide—food, shelter, clothing." They promised unlimited credit.

Baron developed his hobby of wood-carving, whittling ear-plugs.

But nothing could prevent the riots and minor wars, the fall of governments. Oil failed to arrive and transport stopped. The jobless gathered on street corners, wondering: what next?

* * * * * * * *

A club lashed down on Baron's knife-hand and he yelled in agony. A half-brick crashed against his skull and he staggered back, dropping the knife. A fist hit his chest; he stumbled. Hands seized him, pulling him off-balance, dragging him along the road.

He was gasping for air, bruised, with patches of skin bleeding, but still conscious. He heard jeers and laughter and, from time to time, one of them kicked him. He had no hope of fighting them off, so he allowed his body to sag, letting them take his full weight, unable to grasp what they intended.

Why were they dragging him along the road? It seemed pointless. They could do anything they liked with him in the street and nobody would interfere. His skin burned like fire where it continually rubbed against the uneven surface.

They arrived at a cross-roads and what had once been a garage, pumps rusting and long disused. The top of a storage tank had been removed and the tank was open to the air. He was dragged to the edge and pushed over. He fell, with a splash, into an inch of liquid and smelt petrol.

Above him, a ring of faces looked down, mocking. One of the girls produced something Baron hadn't seen for ages and hadn't believed existed any more. A box of matches, stolen from somebody's hoard he imagined.

She struck a match along the side of the box till she got a flame. Then she dropped the lighted match into the liquid surrounding his feet.

* * * * * * * *

The public's initial panic changed to a why-worry? attitude. If they wanted to look after us, why not? Alien machines took over the supermarkets and restocked them. Notices appeared: "Help yourselves—your credit is good with us."

Communications failed as computer networks packed up and nobody bothered to replace them. It was an easy life at first; people relaxed, drifted, lost interest and grew dependent. Responsibility became a meaningless word.

Years passed and gradually supermarket shelves held less variety, just basic stuff; and then less of everything. Whole areas became run-down, schools closed. A new religion devoted to alien worship sprang up; prayers were offered to the new gods, begging food.

Heating again became a matter of collecting wood to burn in an open grate. Hospitals closed, and the death toll rose,

One day Baron met a man who had been a laboratory assistant at a technical college. He was trying to get something started again.

"No-one seems to grasp what is happening," he said, and handed Baron a leaflet. It was hand-written.

These alien machines that change atomic structure are using up the resources of our planet. Soon we shall have no ores to refine into metals, no raw materials to turn into chemicals. They are leaving us with nothing except a huge debt.

* * * * * * * * *

The match fizzled out. Scowling, the girl struck another and dropped it. Baron wasn't worried; the liquid sloshing around his feet was only rain-water.

They got fed up with their failure to start a fire and began to pelt him with stones. Baron retreated to a far corner and sheltered behind an old tin bath someone had dumped.

After a while, the gang lost interest and drifted away. Baron sighed with relief and rubbed his bruises. He measured the depth of the tank with his eye. He had a problem, and didn't feel inclined to shout for help. If the upturned bath would take his weight, he might just reach—

The sky darkened. The air throbbed with sound. Howard Baron looked up as a thousand-mile-long starship descended towards Earth. "Oh, yes," he thought. "Fifty years—of course." The creditors had arrived to collect payment, and he wondered just how they would go about foreclosing a whole planet.

THE PENITENT

by Stephen Laws

"Forgive me Father," said the voice on the other side of the confession-box grille. There was a long pause while Father Krystoff waited for the penitent to finish the phrase. When the voice from the darkness spoke again, it was with a deep and peculiar resonance. It reminded the priest of dripping cellars and heady, full-blooded wine in dark ochre barrels. Kristoff had to struggle to shrug off the image to concentrate on the needs of the penitent. A rather strange image, just from this voice. Which now spoke again:

"For I have sinned."

Father Krystoff became aware of the odour then. In the brief pause during which the outside door of the booth had opened and the invisible penitent had taken his seat in the darkness, the priest hadn't noticed that smell. He shuffled uncomfortably, wondering if Mrs. Perigord—the woman who undertook the voluntary cleaning of the vestry—had been bringing her dachshund into the church again. It wouldn't be the first time that Father Krystoff's shoe had been blessed with the leavings of that foul creature. There was movement at the grille; something like a passing shadow, as if the penitent had thought twice about the visit and had decided to leave. When the priest looked closer, he could see that the movement was actually a smoke-like wisp creeping through the grille from the other side.

Surely the man in the next booth wasn't daring to *smoke* while he asked forgiveness? The odour of the cigarette, cigar, pipe—whatever—was foul.

Like rotten eggs. The voice continued.

"It has been many centuries since my last confession."

"I beg your pardon?"

"No, Father. I have come to beg *your* pardon."

There was something about that voice. It was a suave, cultured voice; there seemed to be a foreign accent, but Krystoff could not place it. Even in those first few, bizarre words, it seemed that there was an *accumulation* of accent—as of many accents fed through some kind of voicebox blender. Something else. A hideous resonance to the words; as if each word, each phrase was being savoured. It was deeply unpleasant.

"Centuries," said Krystoff, trying to ignore the smell of bad eggs. "You said centuries."

"I did," continued the voice from the darkness of the other booth. "My last confession was on April 25th in—as they say—the Year of Our Lord, 1274. I use the phrase advisedly. He has not been My Lord, of course. I have served another."

"I'm sorry. I don't understand. I believe you may have problems that I cannot help you with at this stage, my son. Perhaps I can suggest someone who can provide professional support...?"

"You think I'm insane. You're worried that I might harm you."

"No, not at all."

"It is a prerequisite of the ritual that we do not lie to each other. Is that not right, Father? I have told you only the truth thus far. In honour, and in observance of your faith and your role as a Servant of God, you must hear my confession."

There was displeasure in that voice now. Father Krystoff was afraid. If the person in the other booth was seriously disturbed, might he not fly into a rage if the priest did not go along with his fantasies? There could be the threat of a physical attack. On the other hand, if the priest disavowed him of his fantasies and sent him back out onto the streets, might he not vent his frustrations on an innocent passerby? In faith and duty, he must surely not allow that to happen. Krystoff chose to believe that he was protecting others when he said:

"Very well. Let me hear your confession."

There was a pause on the other side. The smell seemed so much stronger now.

"I was born Anton Garcia Monteros Di Santo on August 21st, 1253 of noble lineage. In my youth I developed a taste for vice, licentiousness and cruelty. My crimes are without number. I have murdered hundreds, and have given orders to my underlings to commit every conceivable atrocity. Personally, I have strangled, eviscerated, blinded, mutilated. I have raped, forcibly buggered and sodomised. I had the eyes of an entire village's children put out with burning irons for an imagined slight. I raped my mother and sisters, and brought about the death of my father by slow poisoning. I took pleasure from slaughtering and flaying alive priests of all faiths."

Silence.

"Are you listening to me, Father?"

"Yes, my son." A slight, nervous cough.

"You think me mad? You believe that I am some wretched creature lost in the cruel fantasies of his mind?"

"I believe you are troubled, yes."

"Then, in faith, you must allow me to continue and give me what I request."

"Go on."

"In my fortieth year, suffering from a terminal wasting illness—caused no doubt by the evil ways which I had embraced—I was visited by the Devil. He promised me everlasting life if I would continue to serve him. In my own way, you see, I had served him so well up until that point. Death would end the career of a promising would-be pupil."

"You are still living then?"

"Yes."

"Then surely you cannot be..."

"A demon? Oh, but yes. You must not believe everything that you've been taught about my kind. To continue the enactment of evil on mankind requires a physical presence. A Deal with the Devil—a Pact, if you will—is really very simple. Continued life, free from the ravages of time, in return for a commitment to pain, horror, and misery."

"And you wish me to absolve you of these sins?"

"Yes."

"How can I, if you are in league with the Evil One?"

"I am human. I was born a Catholic, into the faith. If I have a wish to be absolved, you cannot withhold that from me."

"If you are a Demon, you cannot be human. Therefore the blessing cannot be made."

"I have told you nothing but the truth."

Krystoff paused again. Should he follow through with the madman's logic? Should he give him absolution? Wouldn't that be enough to calm him, give him some peace? Should he keep him talking, find out who he really was and where he lived? Perhaps then he could alert social services to follow-through and give him the help he really needed? Or perhaps he should simply dismiss him, revile him for his blasphemies. If he were to give the blessing, and this madman had committed hideous crimes of some kind, would he feel that the slate had been wiped clean and that he could go out with a fresh conscience and start all over again?

"Touch the grille," said the voice from the other side.

"I beg your pardon—?"

There was a chuckle from beyond the grille. It sounded hideous. "You've confused our roles, Father. If you will allow—put your fingers to the mesh between us. Our fingers will touch. And you will know that I'm telling you the truth."

"This is nonsense. I suggest that you—"

"Touch the mesh!"

Krystoff's hand was even now moving to the grille, the priest unaware that he had made a conscious effort to do so. He watched it move but could not find the will to stop himself.

His fingers brushed the tight criss-cross frame.

On the other side, he had a brief glimpse of something thin and white moving to meet those fingers. And then something deathly cold flowed into his fingertips

Instantly, Krystoff's mind was flooded with scenes of unparalleled horror. The priest convulsed in his seat, retching—but his hand remained fastened to the mesh. A hellish kaleidoscope of images scoured his soul. Atrocities that beggared belief. Cruelty and torture. Anguish, hatred and despair. Blood and torn flesh. A cacophony of monstrous brutalities, bloodlust and obscenity.

When Krystoff's fingertips were released and he slumped back in his seat, he fought to regain his breath. He had been into the Pit—he had seen in those few brief seconds every hideous act that Anton Garcia Monteros Di Santo had committed. And now he could not doubt the truth of the Demon's words.

"My God," breathed Krystoff at last.

"Yes," said the voice. "But not only yours. Mine too, as I was born into the faith."

"Never," moaned Krystoff, trembling fingers moving to his sweat-beaded face. "You foreswore God, made your pact with that Other."

"So have other men over the centuries. They have received absolution for their sins when truly penitent. I too am penitent. I have confessed my crimes. I ask for absolution."

"*Never!* Your presence here, in this church, is a blasphemy."

"Then you refuse me?"

"I refuse you."

"But surely you are a vessel for God? My appeal is to Him, through you. You must act in faith. You have heard my confession. It is heartfelt, and I ask for forgiveness and absolution."

"I refuse you!"

"Did you refuse Heinz Gromheld?"

"What?"

"He was a Nazi Administration Officer in 1942, when you were a young priest in Berlin. His conscience was troubled because of the transportation work he was undertaking at that time. Don't you remember, Krystoff? He acquisitioned several dozen cattle-trucks for the transportation of Jews to Auschwitz, and other concentration camps."

"How can you ...?"

"Know that? What a naive question to ask of someone like me. He came to you, confessed all. You absolved him."

"He was truly penitent."

"He was not, and you know it. He hated the Jews, but he felt that he must go through with the ritual to make sure that he was cleansed. 'Go and sin no more,' you told him. Is that not a part of the rite? Is it not true that forgiveness can only be forthcoming if the penitent agrees to change his ways, promises not to commit the same sins?"

"Yes, but—"

"On leaving your church, with a lighter heart, Gromheld continued in his official duties. He continued to organise the transportation. His conscience no longer worried him."

"That is not a matter for me. That is a matter between

Gromheld and..."

"His Maker? But of course. And is my request not also a matter between my Maker and myself? Once again, you have heard my confession. Once again, I ask for forgiveness."

"I cannot."

"*You* cannot?"

"No," Krystoff's voice was breaking. "I *will* not..."

"Tell me Father," continued the Demon. "You knew what was happening to the Jews then. What did you do about it? How many other confessions did you listen to, how many other absolutions did you give?"

"Leave. For God's sake, leave me in peace."

"You were afraid, weren't you, Father? Afraid for yourself. Afraid to do anything to stop it."

"The Church had ... had..."

"Are you going to say 'an unofficial position'?"

"No, nothing like that. It was just that..."

"And the Rogetson family. Only two years ago. What about Yvonne, Krystoff? What about her father?"

"Oh dear God, leave me alone."

"She came to you first. Begged for you to hear her confession. She was sixteen, and her father had been sexually molesting her since she was six years old. Isn't that true, father? He'd told her that it was alright, but she wasn't sure. Now she could stand it no longer. You listened to her confession, and gave her absolution. In the following week, her father came and asked you for the same forgiveness. Can you remember what you did?"

"Please. Go. I can't stand any more."

"You absolved them both. Yvonne believed that your granting of that forgiveness was a sign of her own sin. Why be forgiven if there was nothing to be forgiven for? She killed herself, didn't she? And you absolved the father, too. Now his conscience is clear, and he does not mourn the slut who was a temptation to him simply by living under the same roof."

"For the last time—*go!*"

"For the last time, I ask for absolution. Unlike those we've discussed, I *will* go and sin no more."

"*Never! Leave this place! I will not absolve you. I WILL*

NOT!"

Suddenly, the smell of brimstone was gone.

Krystoff had buried his face in his hands. Now, he looked back to the grille. There was no other sound from behind it; no suggestion of movement. And yet, instinctively, the priest knew that the presence on the other side had gone. Horror lay thick and vile in the pit of Krystoff's stomach. Breathing out—a loud and heavy sigh—he braced his hands on either side of the confessional and tried to bring himself back to the world that he knew. He could not pretend that this had been some kind of hallucination; that perhaps he had been working too hard and had undergone some kind of localised nervous breakdown. The touch of the Demon had been only too real. Krystoff had been in contact, for the first time in his life, with something truly supernatural—and truly Evil.

The confessional was too confined. He felt as if he might suffocate.

But when he reached for the curtain, he paused. Could this all be some kind of trick? Was that evil thing even now crouched directly outside, waiting for him to emerge? Krystoff closed his eyes, murmured a prayer—and pulled back the curtain.

Beyond, the church lay cold and still.

Anton Garcia Monteros Di Santo had gone back to Hell.

Shuddering, Krystoff clambered from the confessional. His legs felt weak as he staggered down the central aisle of the church, back towards the vestry. He felt strange inside. As if something vile had scoured his very soul. There was a stillness now; a stillness that lay deep and heavy over the pews and the stone walls. It pressed against the stained glass windows, somehow robbing the colour from the vestments of the painted saints. This was unlike the stillness of peace and tranquility that he had so often associated with his church.

At the vestry door, he paused again.

There was much to think about; many questions that he had to ask of himself and about what had happened back there. Too many thoughts now; crowding into his mind, clouding his heart and his soul. Perhaps a glass of sherry would calm his nerves. Krystoff pushed open the door.

And recoiled from the sight that met his eyes on the vestry

floor.

A figure was lying there, sprawled on its side. The arms were outflung, the fingers clutching at the tiled floor as if he could somehow drag himself back to life after the fatal heart attack had smashed him to the floor. The face was a frozen rictus of pain, and for a moment Krystoff had only a vague feeling that he knew who this person could be. This was a priest, like him.

The man had a shock of white hair.

Like him.

The figure had the little finger of his left hand missing.

Like him.

And then Krystoff realised that the face was the same face as his own, albeit frozen in agony.

In that moment, he knew.

He had been dressing himself, preparing for his appointment at the confessional as usual, when the heart attack had felled him. He had died here—had never left the vestry.

The smell of brimstone was suddenly overpowering.

Turning slowly to look back, Krystoff saw that the Church had vanished.

He was no longer standing in the vestry doorway. There was no longer a vestry. No longer a still and silent figure lying on that vestry floor.

Now, he was standing in a vast cavern. Giant stalactites and stalagmites dwarfed him. Gigantic plumes of volcanic flame and ash erupted from the cavern floor, spouting in clouds of molten fury. Lakes of lava bubbled and surged, rivers of molten steel roared and cascaded. Krystoff could see the tiny silhouettes of human figures tumbling and screeching in those lakes and rivers; could hear the constant metallic pounding of gigantic anvils, the explosive hellish roaring of the damned.

A fireball erupted from that inferno. Like some hellish meteorite, it roared from the flames, straight towards him.

Krystoff could not move.

He could only watch as it came on.

And as it came, it began to change. Now it was no longer a fireball, no longer a thing of flames. Now it was a constantly changing maelstrom of eyes and tongues and teeth. It was a huge, monstrous amalgam of everything hellish and obscene in the living world. It was jaws and spider-eyes and hooked beak and razor tongue and blood-sucking, flesh-rending, soul-devouring nightmare. Just at the last, before it arrived, Krystoff heard the deep-echoing voice of Anton Garcia Monteros Di Santo erupting from each of the monstrosity's obscene orifices.

"*Such a shame*," said the would-be penitent. "*That you could not practice what you preach.*"

THE FALLING ELEPHANT

by Philip E. High

My name is Mangrove—Thomas Mangrove. I often wonder if the cleaner who found me near the hospital gave me that name out of spite or whim.

Its traditional round here anyway, find an abandoned untraced baby and the finder has the right to name it. Occasionally I have cursed him, until I was promoted later in life a lot of people called me Swampy.

On the other hand I suppose it shaped my character, one learns to laugh at it and crack back.

To skip a few years, I grew up, passed a lot of exams and became a policeman finally being promoted to detective. I became very good at it because, outside of my training I had a lot of hunches. I say 'hunches' deliberately because if you say 'intuition' people are apt to look at you sideways if you know what I mean.

Before going any further, permit me to make myself plain. I am tall, heavy shouldered and have a big belly but don't be deceived. It's the sort of belly developed by weight lifters and Japanese wrestlers. A wild hopeful punch at it could well numb your arm up to the shoulder.

Returning to my hunches, I often had to cover for them. I had to put in a great deal leg work and legitimate procedures just to hide the fact that I'd got there rather quickly by another route if you follow me.

There was another thing to which I never confessed to Doctors or examiners before joining the force. I think I would still be a civilian if I had ever admitted it. You see, every three months or so —since I was sixteen actually—I have a dream. It is always the same dream, it's very brief and very vivid but it's quite beyond my understanding. No, it doesn't frighten me but I just keep wondering what the hell it means.

I am walking along a narrow defile, walls of rock rising sheer on either side. I have the impression of snow capped mountains near but I don't see them. Perhaps it is only an impression because I am frozen with cold. I sense rather than see other men walking with me but they are only impressions and outlines. Some thirty paces in front me however, and absolutely clear is the most improbable thing of all—an elephant.

In my dream I am not surprised, it has been there just ahead of me for so long that I have accepted it, somehow it has always been there.

Frankly I am so cold and so numb with fatigue that my eyes keep closing and then—then suddenly there is an impact. I hear a man scream terribly and men shouting.

Then briefly, so very briefly I see one really clear picture. Three men hideously crushed on the rock, the elephant lying on its side trumpeting shrilly, then the dream stops as if cut by a knife and I always wake then.

I can only conclude, of course, that the elephant slipped on the icy rocks, crushing the men as it fell.

I cannot explain it, I don't try to explain it, but I call it the falling elephant dream. I have put it in as background to events and a certain relevance to incidents occurring later.

I suppose events really began to take shape when I was called to a presumed murder on White Mountain Lake some twelve kilometres outside the city.

I had been taking a few days rest by the sea and, by the time I got back the body was already on the slab in the mortuary.

I was relieved to see that Dettering was doing the examination. Dettering was brilliant, inspired and quite eccentric but he never missed a trick. I can see him in my mind now, droopy greying moustache, gold-rimmed glasses perched on the end of his nose.

"The deceased was named Proner, a hole starts under his jaw and finishes at the back of his head."

"Yes, I was told it was a shot wound."

"Who told you that?"

"The police surgeon."

Dettering made a short barking sound, which might have been a laugh. "Don't tell me, that would be Midden, of course. Midden makes pronouncements on appearances then passes it on to someone else. Come over here and take a look at the back of the head."

A mere glance was enough; no bullet made that wound. "There's no splintering, no torn flesh."

"Exactly, and, let me assure you, it was not a sword, arrow or spear. Frankly I don't know what did it but I can tell you this, whatever it was it literally burned its way through. The wound is charred, whatever made that wound was white hot. To use a current phrase which, incidentally, I detest—you ain't heard nothing yet."

He sighed and made a gesture towards the body. "Proner was a rich man and I mean rich, he had aircraft and yachts and things. He was on a yacht when he was killed which is another puzzle that I shall come to later. According to his wife he became apprehensive about two months ago. A condition that gradually increased and forced him to take measures against it. He became convinced that someone was out to kill him and he took elaborate precautions against it. He stabilised his yacht in the middle of the lake but even that was not enough. Four smaller vessels went with him full of bodyguards to make sure he stayed safe."

Dettering sighed again. "Even that was not enough, some of those vessels had light anti-aircraft guns but they still got him."

"One of the guards got bribed?"

"Not unless he had psychic powers. Those guards were on the ball all the time and they took frequent photographs for reference purposes."

Dettering extended his hand. "Here is a picture taken approximately eighteen seconds before he died. As you see, he is leaning on the rail looking down at the water."

I saw what he was driving at instantly. "To be hit from that angle, the shot must have come from the sea."

"Precisely, but it solves nothing does it? In point of fact we must assume that the killer swam twenty one miles from shore to the yacht *under water*. He was not only doing the physically impossible but consider the journey in terms of oxygen cylinders plus a weapon of some kind."

I was beginning to feel a definite coldness down my back. I

didn't like the sound or feel of this case at all.

"What sort of weapon do you think it was?" I asked.

He shrugged helplessly. "I thought of a laser but from under water—? I don't know, Tom, I admit this beats me."

I was beaten, too, and worst of all I felt nothing, no intuitive leads, no hunches, nothing.

I wandered down to a quiet part of the lake's shore in the hope that I might find a lead. Marks in the mud such as might be caused by hauling oxygen cylinders around, flipper marks, anything.

As I came back to the road from the water I met a man with a fishing rod.

"No luck, Officer?" he said.

The question brought me up short. "You know me?"

"By sight, yes, and the case is in all the papers, you know."

It was at that moment that many of my hunches came back. Call these reactions what you like but to ignore them is asking trouble twice over. They may seem illogical and completely ignore common sense but one soon learns they pay.

I knew straight away that he had deep ulterior motives and that this was but an opening gambit for something deeper. Also he knew ten times more about this case than he was prepared to tell me.

He was a medium sized man with curly brown hair and a rubbery sort of face which seemed world weary but not unfriendly.

My powers of observation seemed above standard at that moment also.

"You bought that fishing rod as a cover, you know damn all about the subject."

He looked a little shaken. "How the hell do you know that?"

"That's sea rod you're waving around, not exactly the thing for a fresh water lake."

"Clever man." He tossed it away. "Served its purpose for the moment."

"What do you know about this case?"

"Nothing you can pull me in for. I was in Sweden when it took place and I can prove it. I read about it in the papers and arrived by plane in this country this morning."

"What's it to you?? I was getting angry.

"I think I know how it was done and I have a rough idea also who did it."

"I can pull you in for withholding evidence."

"Do that and you'll lose the lot. No, I'll tell you but my way. It's in your interest and mine, either of us could be on that slab tomorrow or the day after."

He touched my shoulder briefly. "I am not your enemy. If you want this case from stage one, meet me at Wilson's Beach within an hour; you're good swimmer but you'll need swimming trunks and a strong belt.

Common sense told me this was absurd and a waste of time but my hunches took over and I went.

* * * * * * * *

The water is very deep at Wilson's Beach and poor performers are not encouraged by the lifeguards.

He was all ready for the water when I arrived and I noticed that his body was well muscled but knocked around quite a bit. There were a lot of long scars on his back and arms.

He handed me a thing that looked like a piece of plastic oxygen mask with the words: "This just fits over the mouth and nose. Don't put it on now or you'll suffocate. Wait until your face is under water then inhale deeply. It takes a lot of nerve to do that but you must obey or you'll be in no end of trouble. Got your belt?"

I handed it to him and he clipped a thing on near the buckle, which looked like a fat fountain pen.

"Right, put on the belt and pull it tight. Put on the mask, go under and take a long deep breath, after which, breathe normally. When you have got used to it, try out my gadget. You press the top once to go, the same point to stop. Give it five minutes. When you come out insert your finger under the mask just below the mouth and it will slide off easily. Remember, don't leave it on."

I suppose that when I dived in, I was acting out of character. Normally I am cautious by nature and, although I have often taken great risks, they have always been calculated.

This time, however, I was really deep before I began to think. I realised the near impossibility of taking a deep breath under water. One's reflexes, common sense and training clamp a sort of lock on the mind to stop you. Yet I was already suffocating, my head seemed to be swelling and my eyesight was blurring. The surface looked a long way above and, in sheer desperation, I sucked wildly at the tiny thimble-full of air that must remain in the mask.

Beautiful fresh air seemed to swirl into my lungs and I sucked desperately for more, gasping and almost choking.

Slowly things returned to normal—no, not normal. I was breathing without effort as if standing on the shore. I had often dived before but with artificial aids, oxygen cylinder and so on, but it was far, far better than that.

I remember the cylinder thing fixed to my belt and pressed the top as instructed. Slowly I began to move forward, no doubt I was being pushed but it felt as if was being pulled. It was no great speed but it was movement. It was, perhaps a slow jog but I found, I could boost this quite a bit if I threw a few normal swimming strokes. I estimated that with a normal fast stroke, I could bring up my speed to a fairly fast run.

He was sitting on the pebbles when I came out of the water and threw me a towel. "Well?"

"It's miraculous." I handed the things back. "Where did you get this bloody stuff?"

He grinned. "To be completely honest, I made it. Fairly simple constructions if you know how."

"What are you—a damned alien or something?"

He looked at me directly, then he said: "No more than you, Detective Mangrove."

It was then I wished I hadn't asked the question, wished I had never thought of it. It felt as if I had leaned suddenly against a wall of ice, numbing my back and freezing my whole body. I found myself shivering; I was torn within myself, wanting to know but terrified to do so.

It was clear he had evidently been in the sea himself and he began to towel himself down.

"In answer to one part of your question," he said. "My father was British, my mother Italian, and I was born in Denver, Colorado."

"I don't even know your damn name and, if I sound angry, I'm blaming myself. I should know better."

"Point taken, but the name is Stanhope—Peter Stanhope. You can check it out later."

I would, of course, but there were more important things on my mind at that moment. I said, savagely: "I don't give a damn if you're a Caribbean Eskimo. If what you say is true, where did you learn an alien technology?"

He smiled; it was a weary kind of smile that for some obscure reason made me feel uneasy. "I didn't learn them, old chum, I *remembered* them."

The feeling of cold was suddenly with me again and I changed the subject quickly. "What were those devices you gave me?"

"Well, the face mask is in effect an artificial gill which is why you were threatened with suffocation out of water—a fish cannot breath out of its natural element. The other thing was a propulsion unit, it takes natural electricity from the water and converts it into energy."

"This has to be settled." I had come to a decision inside myself and was now determined to see the matter through. "You have told me a great deal your way but, in actual truth, you have told me nothing whatever. No single fact links up with another and I am as ignorant as I was before. It is true, of course, that I know how the murder was done but I have no idea who did it and I have nothing on which to hang a case."

He nodded slowly. "Yes, you are right. I think I have shown you enough to prove that I am not a nut case, but a lot of what I have to tell you—well, you will have to prove it yourself."

He made a gesture. "Small restaurant over by the trees there—tell you the whole story over a meal."

He took his damn time and was on his coffee before he spoke. "A lot of people," he said, "believe in reincarnation, no disrespect, for them it may be true but not for myself or many others. They say to themselves, like the reincarnationist, 'I have been here before; I was then a soldier or a serving maid' or whatever."

He paused and sipped his coffee. "It is true, in our case, he or she, was. We have what might be termed a racial memory."

He drained his cup and caught a waiter's attention. "Two more coffees, please. Bring two more in about forty minutes."

He grinned at me sort of lopsidedly. "This going to take me one hell of a long time."

He was suddenly intent. "When I say "I" to you from now on I am not speaking from the first person singular alone. I speak from the memories and experiences of those long dead, from my ancestors, because I can recall the experiences of them all."

He leaned forward slightly. "When I was eighteen I got mixed up in a road accident and until that day I was as normal as any other man. In the hospital my heart stopped and the electrical charge they used to get it going again must have triggered something. When I regained consciousness I remembered it all. I was not frightened, it seemed so natural just as though I had lived so many lives and remembered them all. There were gaps, of course, blanks, unfocussed sequences."

I don't know if he intended to be dramatic but what he said after that almost numbed me. "You wonder why I interested myself in your case—but to be candid I don't give a damn about it. What I needed was *you*! I have a job to do and you are the only man I have ever met capable of backing me up. In the first place we have to take out the remaining *Trarg* and finally knock out the suppressor."

Intellectually I had no idea what he was talking about but emotionally I was almost there before him. Somehow, in some way, he had committed me to a situation from which there was no escape. I had no idea how I knew, but I knew beyond doubt. My body was stiff, I could feel beads of perspiration on my forehead, but I just didn't care.

It was then that I realised that there is more than one side to a hunch. It had been fine for a clue or line of investigation but this was a different thing altogether. This hunch said, follow me and you could lose your life doing so. Intuition was presenting a bill for past favours and I had no choice but to obey.

I resisted an urge to grasp Stanhope by the lapels and drag him across the table. "Shall we stop being cute and evasive, eh? From the beginning if you don't mind."

"Right—but you may not believe it."

"I'll judge that."

He acknowledged a fresh coffee and sighed. "When you asked

me if I was an alien, I replied, 'no more than you.' You see I am—was—an alien, countless generations ago. The difference being that I remember and you do not. If we bring this thing off, you may not remember much but your son or your daughter may begin to—" He let the rest of the sentence hang.

I leaned forward. "Hang on a minute—bring what thing off?"

"I'm coming to that. And I must also add that there have been other sources, people I've met who also remembered bits and pieces before they got rubbed out."

He shook his head sadly then continued. "I—my ancestors—came from another world. It was a planet called Lydren, technically far ahead of this one but culturally way behind. It was not exactly a slave-economy as technical science kept us above that, but we were completely subjugated by our ruling class—the Supremes. They were the masters and they occupied the best parts of the planet and they never let us forget who were the masters. Oh yes, on the surface it looked good, we had our own local and national governments. We had our own police and even, within limitations, our own armed forces."

My anger had evaporated and I found myself caught up in his story.

"What were these Supremes—aliens?"

"I have always supposed so, but my memories do not stretch back far enough to remember their conquest. Obviously it was absolute because their contempt for us was absolute. When they decided to visit one of our areas, everything came to a standstill, including traffic. We were compelled to prostrate ourselves in the road way, and that included women and children. They would walk on the prone bodies rather than around them.

"Good God, were the Supremes human?"

"I don't think so, they were sort of saffron coloured and their eyes were too big. Oh yes, and they had no hair, not as we understand it. It was more like fur and it never varied from person to person. Come to think of it, it was ginger, like a ginger cat, y'know."

"Was there no resistance?" I asked.

He laughed bitterly. "Yes, but they broke it very quickly, not by notices or threats, but by demonstration. As I told you, we had our own technology and we made a nuclear device. We smuggled it piece by piece into one of their cities and primed it to be detonated by remote control a day later. It never responded, despite countless attempts to activate it."

He smiled twistedly. "Six days later, thirty thousand citizens from various parts of the country were rounded up and transported to one of the planet's deserts. They were forced to surround a sand dune, on top of which was the bomb.

"It was then that every television set in the country was blacked out and superimposed by the picture of the bomb."

A voice said: "THIS IS YOUR BOMB. IT IS A VERY DIRTY BOMB. WE HAVE CLEANED IT UP SO THERE IS NO FALL-OUT AND ONLY SHORT-TERM RADIATION. YOU WILL OBSERVE THAT IT NOW WORKS VERY WELL."

"They then detonated the device, taking thirty thousand of our people with it."

I noticed that Stanhope's face was flushed and that his hands were shaking but he kept control of his voice.

"As I said before, it was their withering contempt which reduced resistance. They *knew* we were building it, knew we had smuggled into the city. Then used it to destroy thirty thousand human lives, men, women and children. It was the same whatever we did, *our* poisons, *our* gas, *our* secret weapons were always tried out on us. 'SHALL WE SEE IF YOUR NERVE GAS IS EFFECTIVE? THE FOUR THOUSAND OF YOUR PEOPLE HERE WILL SURELY BEAR WITNESS.'"

Stanhope made a helpless gesture with his hands. "You see how hopeless our resistance became? They made sure we were killing our own kind."

I was beginning to share his anger and in a curious way I had no doubt whatever that he was telling the truth. "What the hell did you do?"

He shrugged. "There was only one avenue left, and that was escape to the nearest habitable planet."

"Clearly you, or some of you, made it to Earth. But how? By spaceship?"

"Well, we couldn't start on a space ship programme, we had neither the time nor places for concealment. No, Tom, my friend, we started to work on matter-transmission. Oh, yes, I can see by your expression that you are as bemused as we were. This kind of science was way above the average man. But our experiments in matter transmission accidentally opened up a whole new field of astro-physics. We discovered that there was another world similar to our own, co-existing in a parallel continuum, a condition our scientists called time/space relative/adjaceny and God knows what else. That world was this one—Earth, *where there had never been an invasion by the Supremes!* We bent all our efforts to perfecting a system of matter transmission that could get our people across the dimensional gulf to this alternate world." He paused to take another sip of his coffee.

His story was incredible, but it explained how the Lydrens had been able to inter-breed with humans. Their world was an alternate version of the Earth, and its people completely human. I snapped back to attention as Stanhope resumed his story.

"It took fifteen years to produce a blue print and another twelve to produce a working model. Our psychiatrists had been having a go too, trying to find a weak spot. They found only one but admitted they had no idea how to use it. *The Supremes were literally obsessed with immortality.* Oh, they were not stupid, they did not expect to see the birth and death of galaxies but they were hoping to multiply their normal life span by fifty. It was an obsession that backfired on us. Where else would they find pigs, the rats, the mice and the monkeys? They rounded us up in hundreds of thousands, in both sexes and all ages."

Stanhope pushed his empty coffee cup away and I saw his fists clench briefly. "Cleanliness and utter sterility was observed in the laboratories but there it stopped. Surgery was conducted without anaesthetics of any kind whatever—nearly one hundred people died in the first hour. When that particular session was over—knowing they had to return to another—over four hundred took their own lives."

"We were over-run with volunteers for our test matter transmissions—anything was better than being dragged back to the laboratories. We needed them, but we grieved, everything worked but re-assembly. We could see our adjacent world for just eight seconds, transmission was a theoretical truth but we just couldn't make it work. Our first volunteers ended up as unresolved energy packets in some dimensional limbo."

Stanhope wiped his face with a handkerchief and took a deep breath. "I could use another coffee," he said.

I ordered, I could do with one myself. It had occurred to me several times to go for something stronger, but fortunately, something held me back. I was to be glad later, a very steady hand would be needed.

He sipped the hot coffee. "We won in the end, first in ones and twos, and later in hundreds. I don't know if the Supremes knew, or knowing, did not care. As far as they were concerned vast numbers were committing racial suicide by hurling themselves from one planet to another. The device would reduce the traveller to his component atoms, project those atoms through time/space/dimensional adjacency programmed to reassemble themselves on this other alternate world."

He lifted his cup and put it down again without drinking. "It was the lesser of two evils, you know. We could take nothing, no ring, nor brooch nor hair pin. We arrived stark naked and unarmed."

He seemed to get a grip on himself and lifted the coffee to his lips again for a short sip. "Over two million got away before the Supremes destroyed the projectors, chiefly I think because a fair part of their guinea pigs had got away."

He laughed shortly. "The most ironic aspect of the whole business however, was the fact that they had succeeded in their experiments—but not in the way they intended. They saw immortality for the individual but we had immortality of *memory*. These are not my recollections, but those of my ancestors which still exist in my mind."

"The Supremes must have realised this and perhaps appreciated that perhaps we saw too much and remembered too much. They decided in the end to do something about it, but they took their time. They sent the *Trarg* after us but they waited four hundred Earth years to do it. As usual, their arrogance was absolute, they sent only four. The *Trarg* by the way were their secret police although, I must add, they were an army in themselves. Each carried a variety of super weapons and a continuously operating suppressor to stop memories developing. Included also was a detector should a dominant gene grow too strong to halt. The unfortunate would be rubbed out immediately, but it was not all success. Some, despite everything, had some memories and took counter measures and one had a crane fall on him. A second was finished by accident, he was in the wrong place at the wrong time. He stopped a very heavy bomb dropped by a Lancaster in World War Two. I have no idea what happened to number three but he ceased to exist about eighty years ago."

He drained the remainder of his coffee. "As you now know, number four is still working. Our friend on the yacht was getting his memory back, he *knew* something was after him."

He drained his cup and pushed it away. "I think I have escaped because the whole lot came back so quickly it failed to register, but there are others—"

He did not finish the sentence but I knew exactly what he meant—tomorrow it could be me.

"What now?" I cursed myself immediately for asking the question because I already knew the answer.

"We'll have to take him out," he said.

I suffered a curious mental reaction. I rejected the action completely. I had been trained to obey rules, to follow procedures. I could not take such unauthorised action. I could not just pick up a weapon and shoot a man on an assumption. I was saying all this, almost believing it, yet deep down I knew it was a smoke screen. No matter what my mouth said I knew I was going to have a go at the bastard.

Stanhope knew it, too. "You finished?" he asked.

I scowled at him. "Are you sure this is the right one?"

"I've been keeping tabs on him for eight years. He's killed twenty-three people. Yes, you could say I'm sure."

"Why now? Why me?"

"I couldn't do this alone. There was never anyone there at the right time to back me up. When I read about you in the papers and checked your record I knew the time was now."

"How will we recognise him?"

"For a start he always wears dark glasses. His eyes are big like those of his masters and might cause comment otherwise. He's tall, wears a false black beard."

I sighed, knowing inside me there was no escape. "Right, what's the plan?"

* * * * * * * * *

The *Trarg* (human cover name unknown) was staying at The Sterling Castle, a very high class hotel indeed. It lay at the end of a long gravel drive and was fronted by pillars and wide white steps. There was also a permanent commissionaire with a peaked cap and long coat. I hated that, I was certain the damn man would get in the way at just the wrong moment.

On either side of the drive there were trees, coloured shrubs, and, on my side, was a small pool with water lilies and a fountain playing in the middle of the water.

The foliage gave us good cover but I was even less happy than when we had started. Stanhope had left certain details to the very last, which I resented.

"You may wonder why I have not tried to take this bastard out myself," he had remarked, "but no one, repeat, *no one*, can take one of these things single-handed. They have a sense device, call it 'a warning of intent.' Approach in absolute innocence and you will pass in safety. Approach in *apparent* innocence and you will be cut down before you can draw breath."

"Thanks very bloody much, most encouraging."

"Yes, but don't you see, its faculty will be *divided.* More than that, it may have grown complacent over the centuries, no one has yet recognised it for what it is."

His assurances had done nothing to increase my confidence and it had not stopped.

"You have to hit the bloody thing in the head first time or we've had it—understood?"

Crouching behind a bush in the grounds of a first class hotel, I understood too well. I could die in these upper class surroundings. My partner clutching a powerful machine pistol could likewise die with me, but that was no consolation. I was a good shot but the rifle seemed to have become unwieldy with waiting, and I was loosing confidence. I hate expending bullets on principle. And now some damn insect was crawling up my right leg to make things worse.

We had been waiting two hours in broad daylight and I felt certain I was going to crack.

When it happened however, everything seemed to fall into place. I was ice cold and in complete command of myself. The forehead of the thing appeared dead centre in my sights and I pulled the trigger. It knew. It never moved a fraction in response but it nearly got both of us.

A tall tree near Stanhope turned briefly to shimmering glowing greenery and fell to dust. Large branches fell off it but they, too, turned to dust before they hit the ground.

Near me there was a *phut!* No louder and no more intrusive than a spot of rain on a hot stove. Yet that sound took out the pond, the water lilies and the fountain and left a hole you could put a truck in.

Thank God my shot had hit the thing in the right place yet, for a second it stood there. It did a curious dance, it stuck its right leg out as if about to do the goose step. Then with its right leg still extended it fell stiffly sideways down the steps like an unseated statue.

I noted with some relief that the commissionaire had escaped unharmed. Probably he had some experience of military action, for he had flung himself to the ground behind a pillar at my first shot.

Stanhope came out of the opposite bushes shaking. "God, that was bloody close, it nearly got us both."

"Yes, yes, put your safety catch on for God's sake." I was shaking inside myself.

"Yeah, yeah—sorry." He sounded on the verge of tears.

We didn't get far, we were not exactly arrested but the atmosphere was hardly friendly. Four escorting police cars did not help the tension either, particularly so as I knew I had broken every rule in the book.

We spent an uncomfortable four hours in a small office and then we were on the move again. We ended up in a huge empty warehouse in which many bright lights had been hung. In the middle of the room was a slab and there was no need to tell what lay on it.

We were urged closer, this time with some violence, and I felt a gun press into my back.

There were quite a few people round the slab, two or three men in coats—Dettering among them, I was glad to note. There was also a tall man with untidy hair in civilian clothes. I never found out who he was but he cut our escort down to insect size.

"What the hell do you people think you're doing? Put those weapons away—*now*—do your hear me?"

He watched them shuffle back, then he said to another uniformed man: "Who is their commanding officer?"

"Midden, I think sir."

He nodded. "I might have known. Have him report to my office in the morning." He turned to Stanhope and me. "Please come forward. I am sure you would like to see this closely."

I had imagined it in the last few hours but it resembled nothing I had thought. I'd had an idea of a sort of robot with metal arms and polished joints, but what I saw frightened me.

Its clothing had been removed and it lay naked on the slab somehow, to me, indecently exposed. I don't know why, because the body was completely sexless with no organs whatever. In other respects it was a human body, slightly green in colour but perfectly built. Only the polished and completely hairless scalp reminded one of a machine.

My shot had got it right between the eyes but the expanding bullet had remained within the skull, which gave some idea of its enormous strength.

A thick greenish liquid was running from the right ear and an obvious chemist already had some in a test tube. "At an educated guess I'd say this liquid had two purposes, first as a lubricant and secondly as a conductor. There's still a lot of power in this thing."

"Trouble is," said Dettering, "it *feels* human." He wabbled the calf of its leg. "Look, just like a man."

Frankly I didn't want to look—the damn thing gave me the creeps. Fortunately Stanhope came forward and approached the man with the untidy hair.

"Have you all the contents of the pockets?"

"Yes, over there on the table."

"Please don't let anyone fool around with them, they're mostly weapons. Your best bet is to take them into a remote desert and have a machine fool around with them."

"How are we going to cover this story?" I asked. "A shoot-out at a plush hotel, an alien—and all these people know."

He smiled thinly and looked about him. "Most of these people will like to keep their jobs and their pensions," he said. "They will fall in line with the official story."

"Which is?"

"You shot a terrorist. The hotel has been cleared and my men have moved. Bomb-making equipment was found both in his room and in his luggage."

Later I said to Stanhope, "What happens now that suppressor is no longer working?"

"Very little for the average person, but for the next generation and the one that follows— One day in the far future we shall remember everything and be ready."

I suppose that ends my report save for one thing—my falling elephant dream. Only it's no longer a dream, I *remember* it, just that fragment. I was marching with an army and I was crossing the Alps. I was crossing the Alps with Hannibal, his armies and his devastating cavalry of battle elephants.